Michelle Douglas has been writing for Mills & Boon since 2007, and believes she has the best job in the world. She lives in a leafy suburb of Newcastle, on Australia's east coast, with her own romantic hero, a house full of dust and books and an eclectic collection of sixties and seventies vinyl. She loves to hear from readers and can be contacted via her website: michelle-douglas.com.

Also by Michelle Douglas

A Deal to Mend Their Marriage
An Unlikely Bride for the Billionaire
The Spanish Tycoon's Takeover
Sarah and the Secret Sheikh
A Baby in His In-Tray
The Million Pound Marriage Deal
Miss Prim's Greek Island Fling
The Maid, the Millionaire and the Baby
Redemption of the Maverick Millionaire
Singapore Fling with the Millionaire

Discover more at millsandboon.co.uk.

SECRET BILLIONAIRE ON HER DOORSTEP

MICHELLE DOUGLAS

MILLS & BOON

First Published in Great Britain 2021
by Mills & Boon, an imprint of HarperCollins*Publishers*
1 London Bridge Street, London, SE1 9GF

www.harpercollins.co.uk

HarperCollins *Publishers*
1st Floor, Watermarque Building, Ringsend Road
Dublin 4, Ireland

© 2021 Michelle Douglas

ISBN: 978-0-263-29174-2

MIX
Paper from
responsible sources
FSC
www.fsc.org **FSC C007454**

For sweet little Mikayla. Welcome to the family.

CHAPTER ONE

OWEN PERRY GLANCED at the clock on the wall of the lawyer's office and then at the lawyer.

Mr Dunkley cleared his throat and adjusted his tie before shuffling the papers on his desk. 'Ms Nicholls only arrived in New York yesterday. It's a long flight from Sydney. She's probably jet-lagged and still finding her feet.'

Owen ground back his impatience. He had no idea why Mr Dunkley was determined to make allowances for Callie Nicholls. He knew as well as Owen did how many letters Frances had sent to Australia. And they both knew exactly how many letters she'd received back in return.

None.

Not one.

With a deep breath Owen forced his jaw to relax and glanced at the envelope on top of the folder in front of him—his godmother's final message to him. He'd brought it along as a reminder, to help him keep his resentment in check and to honour Frances's memory. Frances wouldn't want him telling Callie Nicholls exactly what he thought of her. She wouldn't want him to feel resentful or bitter on her behalf. She'd want him to be professional…and kind.

Unbidden, grief smothered his heart like a pillow pressed to his face, making it hard to breathe. His name, written in Frances's familiar looping handwriting—in fountain pen rather than ballpoint, because she'd had a thing for fountain pens and coloured inks—made him ache.

He wished he could sit in her living room just one last time to argue politics over a game of chess. That, of course, could never happen, and that letter addressed to him had been written in black ink, rather than a whimsical aqua or tangerine, as if to signify the formality of its contents. As if to symbolise death.

Stop being maudlin.

She'd give him a stinging set-down if she could see him now and be privy to his thoughts. But she couldn't and she wasn't. All that was left was her letter.

Darling Owen, you owe me nothing…

He owed her everything! Which was why he'd do what she'd asked rather than give Callie Nicholls a piece of his mind. He'd help this rotten woman however he could, keep an eye on her for as long as she was in New York—which he hoped to God wasn't going to be too long—and he'd be *neighbourly.* Just as Frances had requested.

He might have more enthusiasm for a root canal treatment, but he'd do it anyway. *For Frances.*

The intercom on Mr Dunkley's desk buzzed. 'Ms Nicholls for her ten o'clock appointment.'

Owen's gaze flicked to the clock. Ten twenty-five.

'Send her in,' the lawyer responded.

The door opened and a young woman burst into the room in a flurry of coat-shaking and swift gestures, and for a moment Owen had an impression of colour and sunshine and spring breezes.

'I'm so sorry I'm late!' She unwound a startlingly pink scarf from around her throat. 'New York is insane!'

The lawyer immediately leapt to his feet. Owen did the same, doing all he could to squash the defiance rising through him.

'Does it ever get quiet here?'

He couldn't help himself. 'You're late because of the noise?'

Blue eyes swung to him, a keen intelligence brightening them to the colour of a cobalt glass marble he'd once treasured as a kid.

The corners of a mobile mouth twitched. 'My hotel is right next door to a fire station, and either there are a lot of fires in New York or there's something wrong with their alarm. But, even given my disrupted sleep, I was awake nice and early—bright-eyed and bushy-tailed.'

Bright-eyed? *Tick.* Bushy-tailed…? He refused to let his gaze drop.

'The taxi driver I thought I'd been *so* lucky to hail dropped me three blocks away, swearing black and blue that your offices, Mr Dunkley, were just "right there"—he even pointed to a door—and then charged me twenty dollars for the privilege…which seemed a lot.' She rolled her eyes and set her raspberry-coloured coat on the back of a chair. For the briefest moment her lips tightened. 'I have a feeling I was just taken for a ride—*literally.*'

'Where are you staying?' he asked.

She named a nearby hotel—budget and far from fancy. Not the kind of hotel Owen would want his sister staying at.

'It would've been quicker to walk.'

Her brows rose at his tone and his shoulders knotted. He'd promised to be helpful. Sniping at her wasn't helpful.

Pulling in a breath, he did what he could to temper his tone. 'Your hotel doesn't have the best of reputations. Other arrangements will have to be made for you.'

Those blue eyes narrowed. 'We haven't been introduced.' A small pointed chin lifted—a very determined chin—and a hand was thrust towards him. 'Callie Nicholls.'

He clasped it. 'Owen Perry.' He released it again immediately, his hand burning.

'The executor of my grandmother's will?'

'That's right.' His hands clenched. Why hadn't she written Frances just one letter? Had it really been too much to ask?

'Well, Mr Perry, let me assure you that I'm perfectly capable of making my own arrangements in regard to my accommodation. And whatever else I choose to do while I'm in New York.'

He'd just bet she was.

'So, please, don't trouble yourself on my account.'

She was welcome to stay in a dumpster for all he cared. Still…

'Your grandmother would want you to be comfortable *and* safe for the duration of your stay.'

'That can be solved easily enough,' Mr Dunkley inserted hastily. 'Ms Nicholls, please have a seat.'

They all sat.

'I think it would be prudent for Ms Nicholls to stay in her grandmother's apartment,' said the lawyer.

'No!' Owen's denial was instant, automatic and involuntary.

Both Mr Dunkley and Callie Nicholls stared at him. The non-existent collar of his woollen sweater tightened about his throat. It was just… He couldn't imagine anyone else living upstairs. Didn't *want* to imagine it.

Callie glanced at the lawyer, who swallowed and leaned towards Owen a fraction. 'Why on earth not?'

If Callie moved in he'd no longer be able to go upstairs and sit in the half-dark to breathe in Frances's familiar scent and just…remember her.

'Well…?' Callie prompted now, not unkindly, but with a perplexed furrow ruffling the skin between her eyes.

Damn it all to hell! This woman didn't deserve to profit from Frances in death when she'd refused to come near her in life. He closed his eyes and bit back the howl that pressed against his throat.

This is what Frances wants.

That was what he needed to focus on. Not on how Callie had done Frances wrong.

'The apartment hasn't been touched in over eight weeks. It'll need a thorough airing and cleaning before anyone can move in, and—'

'All taken care of,' Mr Dunkley said with forced cheer. 'I took the liberty of hiring cleaners yesterday. The apartment is ready—' he shrugged '—for whatever Ms Nicholls wishes to do with it.'

Owen ruthlessly pushed all sentimentality away. He couldn't afford it at the moment. 'How *forward-thinking* of you, Mr Dunkley.'

The salient fact was that as soon as Frances's granddaughter signed the paperwork a significant portion of her grandmother's estate would pass to her—including the apartment block her grandmother had lived in. It was a modest complex by New York standards—only eight apartments in total—but it was located in the heart of Greenwich Village, one of the most exclusive neighbourhoods in New York, and worth millions of dollars.

As soon as she put it on the market, he planned to buy it.

They got down to business.

'Your letter informs me that I have inherited a small legacy from my grandmother, Mr Dunkley, which I'll confess was unexpected.'

Owen only just managed to contain a snort.

'But it's terribly exciting. What can you tell me about Frances?'

'She was born Frances Victoria Allbright and grew up in Maine. At the age of nineteen she married Thomas Nicholls, an up-and-coming stockbroker. Thomas tragically drowned over forty years ago, leaving Frances and your mother reasonably well off. Frances, however, never one to rest on her laurels, began playing the stock market. Thomas had apparently taught her everything he knew, and she did rather well for herself.'

As the lawyer spoke Callie moved closer and closer to the edge of her seat, her face glued to Mr Dunkley's.

Avaricious. That was the word that stuck in Owen's mind. It made him sick to the stomach. Frances had deserved so much better.

'She remarried when she was forty-six, but it only lasted four years before ending in an acrimonious divorce.'

'Who did she marry?'

'Richard Bateman…' Mr Dunkley paused, as if waiting for more questions, but when they didn't come he continued. 'A year or so after the divorce she moved from her apartment on the Upper East Side to Greenwich Village, which is where she lived for the last twenty years.'

Which was how Owen had met her. His mother had been Frances's cleaning woman.

Callie leaned forward again. 'Mr Dunkley, these are all interesting facts, but you say you've been my grandmother's lawyer for over thirty years?'

Mr Dunkley removed his glasses. 'What is it you want to know?'

'I want to know what my grandmother was like. What sort of person was she? Did she have a quick temper? Was she fond of cats? Did she have any hobbies? Who were her friends?'

'Your grandmother could be brusque to the point of rudeness, but underneath she had a kind heart,' Owen found himself saying. 'She was fond of neither cats nor small children. She could play a mean game of chess, and she continued to follow the stock market until the day she died. She didn't have many friends—probably because she was insanely private—but those she did have she cherished. She was a philanthropist; she gave generously to a range of charities. And she spent every Christmas alone.'

Callie turned to him, eyes wide and lips parted, as if hungry for his every word. Things inside him tightened.

Things he didn't want to tighten. Or clench. Or burn. She looked the epitome of wholesome small-town goodness—the quintessential girl next door—with her shiny chestnut hair, her wide smile and glowing skin. She looked like the kind of woman who hid nothing—what you saw was what you got.

In other words: trouble.

Owen knew better than to accept anyone at face value. Fiona had taught him that lesson in the most ruthless way possible. He'd base his opinion of Callie on her actions, *not* what she looked like. And, based on her actions so far, she was only out for what she could get.

It took all his strength not to drop his head to his hands. Frances deserved so much better...

The longer Callie stared at the enigmatic and utterly perplexing Owen Perry, the more the breath jammed in her throat. Instinct told her he was the key to everything. This man had *known* her grandmother. If anyone could tell her everything she needed to know, it would be him.

Which was going to be interesting, because every instinct she had told her he didn't like her. How odd... He didn't even know her! Still, in her experience men didn't need an excuse to act either illogically or belligerently, and there was no way on God's green earth she was kowtowing to another privileged male, securely entrenched in his sense of entitlement, so help her God.

She'd find out everything she needed to without his help. She knew how to follow a trail of breadcrumbs to put the past back together. It was what she did. She was a trained historian, for heaven's sake. She didn't need Owen Perry.

'Anything else?' he asked.

While polite, she couldn't help feeling his words were a taunt she didn't understand.

'I'm just envious, that's all. Until recently, I didn't know Frances existed.'

He'd known her grandmother. He sounded fond of her.

'But you knew her—you liked her, I think. What was your relationship to Frances?'

'She was my godmother.'

Godmother? Owen was Frances's *godson?* Her heart, her spine and everything inside her softened. What she'd taken as aversion was grief.

'Oh, Owen, I'm so sorry for your loss. You must miss her a great deal.'

He didn't answer, just glanced away.

Mr Dunkley cleared his throat. 'Let's move on to the legacy, shall we?'

She immediately straightened and turned back to the lawyer, gripping her hands in her lap.

Please, please, please let Frances have left her a letter, explaining why she'd never contacted her. Please, please, please let her have left her a family tree she could finally start to trace.

'Your grandmother was a wealthy woman…'

Automatically she nodded, waiting for the lawyer to present her with the yearned-for letter.

'Your grandmother owned the apartment block she lived in, and she's left that to you—along with a trust fund she started for you when you were born.'

Her pulse quickened. *When she was born?* Had she met her grandmother as a baby?

Both men stared at her expectantly as she shuffled to the very edge of her seat. 'And…?'

The knuckles on Owen's hands turned white. 'You want more?'

'Yes!' Her heart hammered so hard she could barely breathe. 'Didn't she leave me a letter, explaining why she never contacted me? Why would she leave me anything

when she never tried to pursue any kind of relationship with me? Why start a trust fund for me?'

None of it made any sense.

Owen leapt to his feet and started pacing. As if... She frowned. As if he were furious and needed an outlet. His actions made no sense either.

The man's grieving, she told herself.

'Your grandmother didn't leave you a letter,' the lawyer said.

Her heart shrank. No letter? Then—

'But she has left you a comfortable nest egg. The trust fund totals five million dollars.'

As if money made up for not knowing her grandmother, her family. As if— Whoa!

'What?'

'In all, the value of the apartment block and the trust fund totals more than twenty million dollars.'

She gaped at him. It took a moment before she could find her voice. 'You *cannot* be serious? In your letter you told me I'd inherited her apartment—not an entire apartment block. *Twenty million dollars?* That's not a comfortable nest egg. It's...outrageous!'

'Agreed.' Owen's mouth tightened and he flung himself back in his seat. 'It *is* a lot of money, Ms Nicholls.'

'Callie,' she corrected automatically.

Her grandmother had left her ridiculously wealthy. But *why*? None of it made any sense. She wanted to drop her head to her hands. Instead she pushed her shoulders back. A letter would've made things easier, but she wasn't giving up. She'd uncover the mystery of her family's past if it was the last thing she did.

But apparently she'd do it as a wealthy woman.

Only if you keep the money.

The thought filtered into her brain and stuck there.

Did her mother know about all this wealth? She *had*

to know. And yet she'd scorned it throughout the financially difficult years of Callie's childhood. She'd chosen to work hard and struggle alone on her small wage rather than rely on her family's wealth and support. She continued to shun it still.

There had to be a reason for that. A *good* reason.

Her mother had always said rich people made up their own rules—subscribed to a different moral code than the rest of the world, thought they were above everyone else and untouchable. And she hadn't meant it in a flattering way.

It appeared she'd been speaking from experience.

If that was the case then maybe Callie shouldn't accept the legacy? She didn't want to profit from a family that had victimised her mother.

She clenched her hands so hard her fingers started to ache. Dragging air into cramped lungs, she focussed on her one definite course of action and the reason she'd come to New York in the first place—to piece together her family tree. That would help to keep all the emotions at bay— the panic, the hope, the fear. Once she'd traced her forebears she'd be able to put together a step-by-step account of how she'd done so. She was hoping that would earn her a prestigious research position with the TV series *Mystery Family Trees*.

That was all she needed to concentrate on for the moment.

She'd think about the money later.

Besides, once she'd found out the truth she'd know what to do with the money, right?

If she kept it… She swallowed. If she kept it she'd never have to work again. It was like being handed a winning lottery ticket. But she couldn't imagine not working. Not working was wrong on way too many levels.

She'd loved her previous job. For good or ill, it had defined her. A familiar anger fired through her. She pictured the look on Dominic's face when he found out she'd won the TV job—the knowledge that in having her fired from her university position he'd pushed her to win the job he most wanted... Oh, there would be something so Karma-perfect about that.

Her heart slowed and satisfaction warmed her veins. Her success would chafe him from the top of his too-tight shirt collars to the soles of his feet. How sweet that would be.

'Spending the money already, Ms Nicholls?'

The words were said lightly enough, and from some-one else they might even have been teasing, humorous. But there was an edge to them...an edge to Owen Perry. Still, people grieved in different ways. She had to make allowances for that.

'Not yet, Mr Perry. Believe it or not, my mind was far more pleasantly engaged.'

'On?'

She couldn't stop her smile from widening. 'Revenge,' she purred.

And it would serve Dominic right for every self-serving second of his mean-spirited treachery.

Common wisdom said revenge was a dish best served cold, but she wasn't so sure. She was still furious with Dominic, not to mention the head of the history department at her university back home, and revenge fantasies were her greatest source of satisfaction at the moment.

She'd never considered herself particularly hot-headed or grudge-bearing before, but now she knew differently. Now she knew she'd simply never had a reason to be hot-headed. And apparently, given the right set of circumstances, she could hold a grudge like a champion.

'How...delightful.'

Owen Perry's drawl snapped her back. *Concentrate.* She had a family tree to unravel and she needed a trail to follow.

'Mr Dunkley, may I have a copy of the will?'

'Why?'

Owen Perry leaned towards her as he spoke, and for the first time she noticed the innate sensuality in the disturbingly firm set of his mouth. It made things inside her flutter and twitch. With his square jaw and grey eyes, Owen Perry was a disturbingly attractive man.

'Curiosity, I suppose.' And because she was searching for breadcrumbs. But she didn't say that out loud. 'Is there any reason why I shouldn't see the will?'

He sat back with a shake of his head. 'Of course not.'

She did her best to ignore him after that. She had a sneaking suspicion jet-lag was catching up with her. Maybe that was why she'd become so aware of him. Jet-lag could be making her misinterpret the vibe he gave off. After all, the man had no reason whatsoever to dislike her, did he?

It wasn't easy to ignore him. Owen wasn't a diminutive man—he had broad shoulders and a long, lean frame that put him at just over six feet. And he was hard too—muscled, as if he worked out. And all that bristling masculinity vibrated with an intriguing intensity beside her.

She moistened her lips. 'Were there other bequests?'

Other bequests meant there'd be other people she could talk to about Frances—and even if they couldn't tell her about the falling-out that had obviously occurred between Frances and Callie's mother, at least they'd be able to paint a picture of Frances for her.

'There were no other bequests—except to your mother.'

Her heart sank.

The lawyer adjusted his glasses. 'Your grandmother left the rest of her money, along with the family estate in upstate New York, to your mother, Donna Susan Nicholls.'

There was a *family estate*? She straightened. That wasn't just a breadcrumb. That was an entire loaf of bread!

* * *

Callie Nicholls's face lit up at the mention of the family estate and a gargantuan weight slammed down on Owen's shoulders. It took all his strength not to bow under its force. He didn't even have the energy to swear. Clearly twenty million dollars wasn't enough for Frances's granddaughter—she wanted the family estate too. He was glad his godmother wasn't here to witness such a travesty.

'What happens if my mother refuses the bequest?' asked Callie.

It was a circumstance Frances had foreseen. She'd placed a twelve-month timeframe on her daughter's acceptance of her inheritance, with instructions to her lawyer to ignore any letters from Donna refusing the bequest during that time.

Mr Dunkley relayed that information, and then removed his glasses. 'If after that time your mother still refuses her inheritance, it will go to a cats' home.'

Callie turned to Owen. 'You said she didn't like cats.'

It made no sense to him either. He squared his shoulders. 'Nevertheless, I can assure you that the likelihood of winning, if you were to contest the will and seek to have your mother's share of the estate settled on you instead, is extremely unlikely.'

She waved his words away and he had a disturbing impression that she'd barely been listening to him.

'Mr Dunkley, how much money are we talking, here?'

'Five to six times what your grandmother left you. So, somewhere in the region of one hundred to one hundred and twenty million dollars.'

She sagged. 'That's an obscene amount of money... How could I not know my grandmother was one of the richest women in New York?'

'She wasn't. Not by any means,' said the ever-pedantic

Mr Dunkley. 'The richest woman in New York is worth a
hundred times that.'

Owen didn't blame Callie for the look she sent the older
man. He watched with a detached but fascinated interest
as she straightened, wondering what game she planned to
play now.

'Mr Dunkley, do you know what it was my mother and
grandmother fell out about?'

Owen's eyebrows rose. Was she hoping to heal that
breach and inherit that 'obscene amount of money' in turn
when her mother died?

Mr Dunkley pursed his lips into a prim line. 'Your
grandmother never took me into her confidence.'

She turned to Owen and raised an eyebrow, and for a
disconcerting moment he wondered if he'd misjudged her.
All he could see in her face was bafflement. There wasn't
an ounce of guile, and no—

Don't be an idiot. It was simply part of an act. The same
kind of charade Fiona had played.

'What about you, Mr Perry? Do you have any idea?'

Owen shook his head. He had no idea what had happened between Frances and her family.

Mr Dunkley shuffled some papers. 'Let's get this paperwork done, shall we?'

It took a ridiculously short amount of time to dispose of
a fifth of Frances's estate. A few signatures, Callie's bank
account details, and the key to Frances's apartment promised in the next day or two. A fifth of Frances's life—gone,
just like that.

A fist reached into Owen's chest and squeezed hard. It
should be more difficult. It should take longer. Callie Nicholls should be forced to jump through hoops and prove her
worth. There should be…

There should be more than this clinical practicality!

Callie Nicholls should be damn well *grateful* to her

grandmother. And she should've given Frances the time of day when her grandmother had been alive. She could've answered at least one measly letter. Was it too much to ask in exchange for twenty million dollars?

They left the lawyer's office together. As they took the elevator to the ground floor his conscience chafed him. Damn it all to hell! He was supposed to be fulfilling his promise to Frances.

When they reached the foyer he pulled his business card from his pocket and handed it to her. She raised a dubious eyebrow, and for some reason that set his teeth on edge.

'My card,' he said. 'If you need anything while you're in New York, I hope you'll contact me. I'll help in whatever way I can.'

Very slowly, she reached out and plucked it from his fingers, careful not to touch him. 'That's surprisingly kind of you.'

He deserved that.

Her lips pursed and her eyes suddenly narrowed. 'You say you were my grandmother's godson?'

He lifted what he knew was a crushingly supercilious eyebrow, but he couldn't help it. 'Would you like to see my baptism certificate?'

Just for a moment humour made her eyes sparkle. 'You've no idea how tempted I am to say yes to that.'

When her lips curved up like that, they looked suddenly and irresistibly kissable. Her humour, and the direction of his thoughts, took him entirely by surprise. He had to bite back a smile—totally inappropriate. He had no intention of falling for this woman's charm. A charm no doubt honed and practised to take in gullible fools like him.

She slipped his card into her handbag. 'If you're Frances's godson,' she said slowly, 'and the only bequests she left in her will were for my mother and me…'

He frowned. Where was she going with this?

'Do I need to make you some kind of monetary reparation? If you were expecting something and didn't receive it…' She shrugged. 'That would explain it.'

He clenched his hands so hard he started to shake. Was money all this woman could think about?

'Explain what?' he managed to ask in a credibly even tone. He, for one, *would* do Frances proud.

'The distinct impression I get that you don't like me.'

He dragged in a breath. Evidently he'd have to work harder if he truly wanted to do Frances proud. 'I'm sorry if that's the impression I've given you. It's been a…difficult day.'

Her face softened.

'And, no, you do *not* need to make me any financial recompense. I would refuse it if it were offered. So please save yourself the bother and me the offence. Frances gave me everything I needed while she was alive.'

He didn't need any handouts from the likes of Callie Nicholls! Frances had saved both him and his mother. She'd given him a top-notch education that he'd forever be grateful for. But more than that she'd given him her love and support. Nothing could replace that. *Nothing*.

Her lips thinned and her eyes narrowed. 'I see. Well… It was a…*pleasure* to meet you, Mr Perry.'

Her inflection told him she meant the exact opposite.

Without another word she turned and stalked out onto the busy downtown street, head held high and with a sway to her hips that, despite his fiercest efforts, had male appreciation heating his blood.

The moment she was out of sight he threw himself down onto one of the foyer's strategically placed sofas, raking both hands back through his hair. That could've gone better…

His phone rang, jolting him back into the present. It was the new intern he'd recently taken on. Christopher used a wheelchair, and worked remotely from his home in Ohio. Owen talked him through a coding issue, channelling some much-needed patience.

No sooner had he ended the call, however, than his phone rang again. He didn't recognise the number, and hesitated to answer it, but eventually he pressed it to his ear and barked a curt, 'Hello?'

'I'm sorry to trouble you, Mr Perry, especially so soon after having met with you, but you did tell me to call if I should need any assistance...'

Callie Nicholls!

Darling Owen, help her in whatever fashion she needs.

'And I meant it. How can I help?'

'My hotel room has been burgled. Naturally, I'd prefer not to stay here now. I've just spoken to Mr Dunkley and he said you have a key to Frances's apartment. I mean, he has one too, but it's currently still with the cleaning company he hired. And while he's expecting them to drop it off this afternoon...'

Her words petered out, as if she'd run out of energy, and a sudden wave of compassion threaded through him.

He deliberately hardened his heart. Concern was reasonable, but instinct warned him against anything more benevolent or generous.

'I'll be right there.'

CHAPTER TWO

CALLIE LEAPT OUT of the armchair in her hotel's misleadingly respectable foyer, unable to sit still for another moment. As much as she hated to admit it, Owen Perry had been right. This hotel was a disaster. Beyond its shabby-grand foyer, with its chintz armchairs and ostentatious chandelier, the rooms were poky and plain. And, while Callie had never considered herself a stickler, they weren't scrupulously clean either.

She could make do with poky quarters and a bit of dust—she'd once lived in student digs, for heaven's sake—but the appalling lack of security was scandalous. She should've done more research before booking...read some reviews, made some comparisons.

She huffed out a laugh. *Yeah, right.* She'd been knocked so far sideways on receiving the registered letter notifying her of her grandmother's death that it was extraordinary she'd managed to arrange flights and accommodation in the first place.

Her pulse skittered. She had a *grandmother*.

Correction—she'd *had* a grandmother.

She folded her arms tight. And now she'd not only lost her grandmother, but every darn thing she'd brought with her to New York bar the clothes on her back and the handbag slung over her shoulder. Said handbag didn't contain all that much either, as she'd heard all the usual horror stories about tourists having their bags snatched, yada-yada-yada, so she'd deliberately left most of her money and valuables in the safe in her room, thinking they'd be...well, *safe*!

Apparently she'd been wrong about that as well.

'Callie?'

A warm and ridiculously comforting voice had her swinging around. *Owen*. While her sixth sense still told her he didn't like her, the sympathy in his face and the concern alive in his eyes had her fighting the urge to throw herself into his rather capable-looking arms to sob her heart out and let him fix everything.

She rolled her shoulders. That was just the jet-lag talking. She wasn't a sobber. And she never abdicated responsibility. Not any more.

Her initial instinct had warned her to stay on her guard around Owen, and she meant to listen to it. The man had obviously fleeced Frances out of as much money as he could while the poor woman had been alive. He couldn't be trusted.

Her fingernails made half-moons in her palms. 'That was quick. You've obviously mastered the flagging a cab thing better than me.' Things inside her pulled tight. 'So... would you like to gloat?'

His brows drew together and her words seemed suddenly small-minded and petty.

'Gloat?' he repeated.

'You told me this hotel wasn't up to scratch. And you've been proved right.'

His lips thinned as he glanced around the foyer—almost as if he was trying to pinpoint her robbers, though they'd be long gone.

'I'd have rather been proved wrong.' His gaze returned to hers with a sudden and startling sharpness. 'You took offence when I suggested you should change hotels. Why?'

'Because it wasn't a suggestion—it was an instruction. It sounded patronising, and it implied that I couldn't look after myself.'

He was silent for a moment, his lips pursed, as if he was replaying their earlier conversation in his mind. Eventually he nodded. 'You're right. It did. I apologise. I didn't mean it to.'

Okay. Um…wow…

'I'm glad you called. I'm the most logical person to help you as I'm the one who has a spare key to your grandmother's apartment.' He nodded, more to himself than her. 'So, yes, I'm the logical person to escort you there.'

He'd used the word *logical* twice. Right…they were going to be *logical*, then.

She made a 'logical' decision not to ask why he was the keeper of the key—she wasn't sure she wanted to know. She just wanted to get away from this hotel. It was starting to give her the heebie-jeebies.

'The thieves took everything?' he asked.

'Right down to my toothbrush.'

'Was anything of value taken?' He raised his hands. 'And, before you take offence, I'm not implying that your clothes or suitcases aren't valuable.'

'But they can be easily replaced,' she agreed. 'As can my toiletries. Can you believe they didn't leave me a single lipstick? They even took my shampoo.' The sheer thoroughness of the robbery astounded her. 'The room was picked clean. I didn't want to carry too much cash, or keep all my cards on me—or my passport—so I put them in the room safe.'

'And, let me guess, the safe is gone?'

'Bingo. I've cancelled the cards and contacted the embassy.' She glared across at the reception desk. 'I asked the hotel if there was some way they could give me some cash against my card. I mean, they have my credit card details and they have charged me for my stay, but that's too hard, apparently, and God forbid they should actually put themselves out to help a guest.'

'They *charged* you?'

That had irked her too. 'Technically, I did stay the night.'

'Excuse me for a moment.'

He strode across to the reception desk without waiting for her reply. She watched, wondering if he'd have any more luck than she'd had. Words were exchanged and, while she couldn't make them out, the tone Owen used had her biting back a smile. The manager was summoned and before she'd realised what had happened she was being offered an apology and her bill was being refunded—in cash—along with a series of vouchers to an array of New York tourist attractions thrust into her hands.

'How did you manage that?'

He didn't answer, just ushered her out of the hotel. 'Let's get you settled at your grandmother's.'

Ten minutes later she found herself standing in the small entrance foyer of an unprepossessing apartment building. He pointed to the stairs. 'We're heading to the top.'

They trudged up to the fifth floor. 'These stairs must've become difficult for Frances as she got older.' Callie was breathing hard herself. 'How did she manage them?'

'She didn't.'

'There's a lift?'

His lips pressed into a tight line. 'She didn't go out.'

Something he'd said back in the lawyer's office clicked into place. 'She was a recluse?'

'Of sorts.'

That wasn't going to help her breadcrumb trail. She opened her mouth, but instinct warned her that questioning him further would be fruitless, so she snapped it shut again.

Unlocking the door, he ushered her in, but didn't follow. His grey eyes had darkened and she sensed a storm building in their depths.

'You're not coming in?' she asked.

Dear God, did she have to sound so *needy*? She wasn't some distressed damsel.

Chin up. Shoulders back.

'How thoughtless of me. You must be busy…probably need to get back to work. I'm sorry to—'

'There's nowhere I need to be. I'm not working today.'

Uh-huh… Right, then…

She gestured behind her at the apartment. 'Then would you like to come in?'

He let out a long breath, coloured with something she couldn't put her finger on. What she did know was that it wasn't enthusiasm.

'Fine.' He marched in. 'I'll put the kettle on.'

For a moment she wanted to tell him to forget about it and go home, where he could be a grump on his own time rather than hers. But she bit the words back. The man had come to her aid without a murmur of complaint. He'd prevented a bad situation from getting worse. He didn't deserve her rudeness.

The apartment wasn't cavernous. Callie had figured anyone with as much money as Frances would live in something wildly opulent, but while it was comfortable, the apartment was by no means luxurious. It was also painted a dull brown that certainly didn't show it off to its best advantage.

The front door opened onto a large room with one corner given over to a kitchen and dining area. To the left of that two three-seater sofas stood at right angles to each other on an enormous Persian rug. An entertainment unit with a TV and top-of-the-line stereo system rested against the far wall. Various dressers, side tables and bookcases were scattered around the room. It was unsophisticated, but comfortable, and not what she'd been expecting.

Owen pointed at the two doors that stood either side of the entertainment unit. 'They're the bedrooms.'

She peeked inside the nearest, which had a view over the street. It had evidently been Frances's and she closed the door hastily, feeling like an intruder. The other, exactly the same size, was a guest room. She'd sleep there. It had a balcony, which was a bonus, even if it did only look out onto the backs of other apartment buildings.

'And the bathroom is on the other side of the kitchen wall.'

Just for completeness, she stuck her nose inside there as well. It was clean, and more generous than the bathroom she'd had at the hotel. It even had a bathtub. She made a mental note to grab some bath salts.

When she emerged back into the main living area, Owen handed her a steaming mug. 'It's black, I'm afraid. There's no milk. I'll organise a few staples to be delivered.'

She opened her mouth automatically to refuse, but closed it again. Who knew how long would be before she had access to her own money again? 'Please keep a record of all that I owe you. I'll settle with you as soon as I can.'

He gestured at the room. 'What do you think?'

The question was freighted with far more meaning than she could decipher. It made her hesitate, but eventually she shrugged. 'It's comfortable. I like it.'

'You hate it.'

'Not true.'

It was just… The apartment might be generous by New York standards, but it was far too small for someone to have remained cooped up there as a recluse.

'Did my grandmother die here?'

He sipped his coffee, those grey eyes cool and reserved once more. 'Would it bother you if she had?'

It wasn't her grandmother's death that bothered her. It was the way she'd chosen to live her life. She sipped her coffee too. It was far stronger than she was used to, but she refused to grimace.

'You just answered a question with a question, so I'm guessing that's a yes.'

She wished she could get a handle on him…read him better. Just a tiny little bit would help.

'I'm not squeamish about staying in a place that some-body has died in.' She sent him an apologetic smile, because the words felt as if they should come with an apology. 'I'd just like to know, that's all.'

'Frances was taken ill here, but she died in hospital.' He paused, as if fighting with himself. 'If you're not squea-mish, why ask?'

And there it was—the latent hostility that rose and bris-tled from him like a wolf's hackles. It had raised its head a couple of times in the lawyer's office, and she knew now that she hadn't imagined it.

She took another sip of her drink, her pulse picking up speed. 'Because I know nothing about my grandmother's last days.' And she needed to find out everything she could about the woman. 'Was she alone?'

She wasn't asking just in the hope of finding a contact who could help her fill in all the blanks in her family tree either. She sincerely hoped Frances hadn't died alone. No-body should die alone.

'Did she have someone with her at the end?'

'Yes.'

She straightened when she realised who that person had been. 'You?'

'Yes.'

After leaving the lawyer's office, she'd had every inten-tion of having nothing more to do with Owen Perry, but it was beginning to dawn on her that he might be the only person who could tell her all she needed to know.

She refused to let her shoulders sag. Refused to let her sudden exhaustion show. 'Why don't you want me stay-ing here?' The question blurted from her, but she needed to know.

His mouth tightened. 'Do you mind if we take care of a few housekeeping things before I answer that?'

'Housekeeping?'

He lifted his phone and punched in a number. 'Rachel, I need a favour. I've an acquaintance who's just arrived from Australia and, long story short, she finds herself with nothing except the clothes she's standing up in.'

And twenty million dollars she wanted to say, just to annoy him. Though she didn't know why she wanted to annoy him. Except his using the word *acquaintance* had stung. It shouldn't have. It was the truth. But that hadn't stopped it from sounding so damn dismissive.

'That's exactly what I'm hoping.'

There was a pause while he listened to the person on the other end.

'So if I text you her picture you'll be able to gauge her size and have some essentials sent round?'

There was another pause.

'Excellent. Charge it to the company credit card.'

He gave the address of the apartment and then rang off.

'May I?' He held up his phone as if to take her photograph.

She tried not to focus on the way the thin woollen material of his jumper pulled taut across a pair of tantalisingly broad shoulders, or how the charcoal colour brought out the colour of his eyes.

'Why don't I just tell you my sizes?'

'They can be different between countries. Rachel is a wizard. She'll take one look at your picture and know your size.'

She nodded. She did need some basic essentials ASAP, and it was just easier to go with the flow.

He took the photo and then sent it to this unknown Rachel.

She stared at him. And then realised she was staring, so

forced her attention back to her coffee. 'What do you do? For work, I mean.'

His gaze turned sharp. 'Why?'

'Why do you have to be so suspicious?' She set down her mug. 'All I want to know is if your boss is going to be okay with you charging personal items—*female* personal items—to your company credit card. I've caused you enough inconvenience as it is.'

He swung away, stowing his phone in his back pocket. 'I'm a software engineer. I develop programs and apps for mobile devices. There won't be any trouble.'

Lucky him. His employer was evidently far more understanding and fair-minded than hers had been. Still, Owen was a man, and from where she was standing it seemed there were different rules for men.

'Next,' he said, his voice businesslike as he reached for his wallet, 'how much cash do you have on you?'

She wrenched her gaze from his strong thighs. Owen made jeans and a jumper—*sweater* in New York, she corrected herself—look like a work of art.

'Oh, please, put that away! Thank you, Owen, but you've already done enough. I'm very grateful, but I have enough cash to last me a few days.' *If she was frugal.* 'I promise,' she added, when he opened his mouth. 'Especially with the refund you scored for me back at the hotel. And if I find I'm running low I'll call on Mr Dunkley and make him earn the no-doubt outrageous fees he's been charging Frances all these years.'

'A fee he's now charging you.'

'Is there any other "housekeeping" we need to take care of?'

'I don't think so.' His nostrils flared. 'Everything in this apartment now belongs to you. You're free to do with it what you will.'

And he hated that fact. That much was obvious.

'Are you going to answer my question now?'

He turned away, his jaw clenching. 'I didn't want you staying here because—' He raked a hand through his hair, before swinging back. 'Look, it's not personal, okay? *I miss Frances.*'

His intensity took her off guard. 'Okay...'

'And over the last few weeks I've been letting myself in here and sitting down in my usual spot on the sofa to watch *Law and Order*, like I used to do with her when she was alive. It...' He trailed off with an impatient shrug.

Her heart burned, because she could see the grief stamped on his face and, despite all her suspicions, she knew it wasn't feigned. 'It made you miss her less?'

'Not really. It was a small comfort, that's all.'

And now she'd taken that away from him. She should leave...stay somewhere else. 'I guess it's too much to hope that there's a vacant apartment in the building?'

'They're all tenanted.'

Of course they were.

'What?' he demanded, when she continued to stare at him.

'I just don't get you. You obviously cared about Frances and yet you...'

'I *what*?' he bit out.

'Took her for a ride—took advantage of her. Or is all of this resentment and hostility...' she waved a hand at him '...because your meal ticket has run out?'

Owen's head rocked back. What the hell...? *Meal ticket?* He didn't need a meal ticket. He was a *giver* of meal tickets.

But Callie obviously didn't know that. She had no idea who he was—that he was the name and the brains behind Perry Apps. He was more than happy for it to stay that way too. Avarice was this woman's middle name. He didn't need the hassle of yet another gold-digging woman trying to infiltrate his life and his heart. Callie was pretty, but she wasn't *that* pretty.

Are you sure?

He rolled his shoulders, angry with himself. He might have a weakness for her particular brand of fresh-faced wholesomeness, but he was neither a fool nor a masochist.

'You're accusing me of financially profiting from your grandmother, when it's *you* who has inherited twenty million dollars?'

'The fact that I've inherited part of Frances's estate has seriously irked you—'

You bet it had!

'Despite the fact I couldn't possibly have taken advantage of someone I'd never met and had no contact with…'

Sing another song, sunshine.

Her hands clenched, as if she could read the scorn in his heart. 'You *told* me you'd fleeced her.'

What?

'When?'

'When you said, *"Frances gave me everything I needed while she was alive"*!' she shouted at him.

He stilled at the fury in her eyes. He tried telling himself her anger was because she thought he'd stolen what was hers, but instinct told him otherwise.

Instinct? *Ha!* What use were instincts? They'd proved so monumentally fallible where Fiona was concerned that they couldn't be trusted or listened to or taken into account. He'd honestly thought Fiona had loved him for himself. Not his money.

A vice tightened about his chest until he could barely breathe. If she'd succeeded in her plan he'd have been bound for the rest of his life to a ruthless, rapacious woman he couldn't respect. He'd had a narrow escape. And it had been dumb luck, not reasoned deduction, that had revealed

Fiona for the woman she was rather than the woman she'd wanted him to believe her to be.

Instincts had no place in his world view any more, or in his decision-making, or in any course of action he embarked upon. He wasn't making the same mistake twice. The only thing he'd rely on now was evidence and cold hard facts.

And what *were* the facts? From the sparks flying from Callie's eyes and the way her hands had clenched in white-knuckled violence… Callie was furious. *Fact.*

'It seems like you preyed on a lonely old woman, which is a truly despicable thing to do.'

It would be if it were true.

Callie slammed her hands to her hips. She wasn't some tiny, fragile-boned pixie girl—she had curves. Curves that had his groin tightening and a thirst rising through him. She had muscles too, as if she worked out or played sport. She didn't have a large build, but he had a feeling that if she threw a punch there'd be enough force behind it to wind a guy.

And she looked as if she'd like nothing better than to punch *him*. The realisation lightened some of the weight that engulfed him.

Then her shoulders lost some of their tightness. 'And yet you were with her when she died. You didn't let her die alone.' She cocked her head to one side and surveyed him. 'Which I guess makes you a wolf with a conscience.'

He was tempted to let her continue believing the worst. He neither needed nor wanted her good opinion. At that precise moment, though, Frances's face rose in his mind, with that knowing eyebrow raised as if to ask, *Really?* and he found himself huffing out a breath.

'You managed to put the worst possible interpretation on those words, didn't you?'

Her chin lowered a notch. 'What *did* you mean, then?'

He drained the rest of his coffee and then strode across

to the sofa and sat. In Frances's seat. Because he couldn't bear the thought of seeing anyone else in it—especially if that someone was her undutiful granddaughter. She hesitated and then took a seat too, at the other end of the sofa, curled up against its arm in a spot where he couldn't remember anyone ever sitting.

'My mother was Frances's cleaning woman. I was four when Mom starting cleaning for her—not at school yet—so my mother often had to bring me to work with her. The first time I came here, Frances taught me to play checkers.'

Callie smoothed her hands across her skirt and for a moment all he could see were her knees—really pretty knees. He shook himself. Pretty knees? Was he losing the plot?

'I thought you said she didn't like small children?'

'For some reason she made an exception for me.' For which he'd always considered himself blessed. 'My father was an alcoholic, and sometimes violent.'

Callie's gaze speared his and he found himself shrugging.

'He never hit my mother or me, but he punched holes in walls, broke dinner plates, threw things. We knew it was only a matter of time.'

As a little kid, he'd lived in fear of his father. It wasn't something he liked to dwell on.

'Frances helped my mother leave him—gave her cheap accommodation here in this apartment block. She took an interest in us—in me.' Loss hollowed out his stomach. 'She was the grandmother I never had.'

Callie sucked her bottom lip into her mouth. When she released it, it was plump and red from where she'd worried at it…and disturbingly fascinating.

'Where's your father now?' she asked.

'As soon as he realised he couldn't force my mother to come back, he told us we were dead to him. We haven't seen him since.'

'So… Frances, your mother and you were a family of sorts?'

They had been, and he didn't have enough family to be blasé about losing any of their number.

He refused to allow his attention to fix on her lips.

'She paid my college tuition fees. Without the benefit of that education I'd be pulling beers in some bar or lugging bricks around a building site. And, while there's absolutely nothing wrong with either of those things, she gave me the opportunity to find my place in the world. That education opened doors that had been previously shut to me.'

Her brow cleared. '*That's* what you meant when you said she'd given you everything you needed while she was alive?'

Exactly.

'I'm glad.' But she didn't smile. She stared across the room, her brow once again furrowed.

Owen… Frances's voice sounded a warning through his mind.

He ground his teeth together. 'What's wrong? You don't look pleased?'

Her gaze swung back to his. 'You and your mother looked after Frances?'

'We all looked after each other.'

She made a noise of frustration, lifting her hands. 'So why didn't she leave her money—her estate—to the two of you, instead of me and my mother?'

'We didn't want her money!' His throat burned. 'That's not what our relationship was based on.' He leaned towards her. 'But, speaking of despicable…' He was incapable of keeping the edge from his voice.

Their gazes clashed and she raised an eyebrow in exactly the same way Frances used to do, and for a moment he couldn't speak.

'What have I done that's despicable?' she asked. 'Besides being late for this morning's meeting and choosing the wrong hotel?'

Don't raise your voice. Don't yell. Don't roar at her that Frances deserved better.

'You said you wanted revenge on Frances.'

Her jaw dropped. 'I said no such thing!'

She wanted to deny it? He'd been there!

'Just after Mr Dunkley told you about the inheritance.' He dragged in a breath. 'You were smiling, and I asked you if you were already spending the money.'

She stared back, and then her face cleared. 'I wasn't referring to my grandmother when I said I wanted revenge.'

'Who were you referring to?'

'None of your business.'

Bizarrely, he had to fight a smile.

'Until a couple of weeks ago I didn't even know my grandmother existed. Why on earth would I want revenge on her?' She slumped back. 'She's given me all this money. What I don't understand is why she never tried to contact me when she was alive.'

He shot to his feet. 'Can we just cut that pretence? I know the truth.'

She stared at him and rose too. Something had changed in the depths of her eyes—the blue was neither so brilliant now, nor so clear.

'Would you care to explain that? Are you saying Frances *did* try to contact me?'

He'd just told her how close he and Frances had been. Did she honestly think him ignorant of the letters? Hell, he'd posted an awful lot of them himself.

He strode across to the antique dresser on the far wall and pulled open the top drawer, gesturing for Callie to come and take a look. The moment she drew near, the scent of spring flowers filled his senses. He backed up a step. Callie might look pretty, and she might smell pretty, but her heart was as black as pitch.

He kept his face trained on hers as she drew out the letters—hundreds of them—some of them addressed to Callie and others to her mother. She took them back to the sofa and stared at them. With her lower lip caught between her teeth, she sorted through them, checking the dates on the postmarks and collating them into two piles—hers and Donna's.

Eventually she glanced up at him, her eyes suspiciously bright. 'She wrote to me…'

He didn't bother dignifying that with an answer.

Her lips twisted. 'Oh, that's right. You're being a typical discerning male. I suppose it's *logical* to think that because they were returned *I* was the one who returned them.'

He blinked, felt something scratching through his chest. Was it possible he'd read her wrong? She didn't look guilty. Unlike Fiona when he'd caught her out in her lies. Of course that could simply mean she was a better actress than Fiona.

Or it could mean you have this wrong.

Facts. He needed to focus on facts.

She drew a pen and a scrap of paper from her handbag, scrawled something on it and then held it out to him. Forcing his frozen legs to move, he took it. She'd written *Return to Sender.* Then she handed him one of the letters addressed to her.

He studied the handwriting. With a mouth that had gone as dry as the Arizona desert, he reached for one of the letters addressed to Donna. The instruction on both letters was written in the same hand, but it was different from the sample that Callie had written on the scrap of paper.

He lowered himself back down to the sofa. 'Your mother returned all of these?'

He didn't know why he asked the question when the evidence in front of him provided the answer.

'So it would seem.'

'So when you said you weren't aware of your grand-mother's existence…'

'I wasn't lying.'

He rubbed the back of his neck. 'I didn't believe you.'

She shrugged, gesturing at the letters. 'I can see why you came to the conclusion you did.'

They were both quiet for several long moments. Eventually she glanced up. 'You thought *that* of me—' she pointed to the letters '—and yet you still came to my rescue at the hotel today. Why?'

He hesitated, reluctant to tell her the truth, but suspecting he owed it to her. 'I promised Frances I would provide you with every assistance if you should ever come to New York.'

'And, despite how you felt about me, you were determined to carry out her wishes.' She tapped a finger against her lips. 'Which turned out lucky for me.'

'Callie, I'm sorry. I—'

She waved his apology away. 'It doesn't matter.' Her accompanying smile was strained. 'It at least explains why I sensed you didn't like me.'

Her eyes clouded as they travelled back to the letters and Owen's temples throbbed. Her mother had deliberately kept them from her. Why would she do that? There must have been seriously bad blood between the two women. It was beyond him to understand why Donna had refused to patch things up when Frances had proffered an olive branch, though. They were *family*! Family should mean something.

'Did Frances ever speak about my mother and me?'

He shook his head. And he'd never asked. He'd known that Frances had been married twice, and that she had a daughter, but his mother had warned him never to pry into Frances's affairs. They'd been so grateful to her, and neither of them had wanted to cause her pain or discomfort. It had been unspoken, but they'd both known that Frances's family was the one topic that was off-limits.

He'd respected her privacy. Wishing he'd done otherwise now was pointless. She'd never have told him anything anyway, and he'd have only vexed her.

'I guess these now belong to me.' Callie gathered her letters into a pile. 'Which means I'm free to read them.'

He gestured at Donna's letters as Callie collected them up and returned them to the drawer. 'What are you going to do with those?'

'I haven't a clue. I've a feeling my mother should read them.'

'But…?'

She swung round and the light from the windows caught the auburn highlights in her hair. 'My mother isn't an unreasonable woman, Owen. She's…lovely. She's smart and fun and I respect her. We're close.' She moved back to trace a finger across the letters. 'I'm beyond shocked to find she's kept these from me. It goes against everything I know about her.'

He rested his elbows on his knees, searching her face. 'What are you saying?'

'I'm saying she must have a very good reason for not wanting me ever to meet or even know about Frances.'

He stiffened. 'Then she'd be wrong.'

They were both suddenly on their feet, eyes flashing and breathing hard.

'Of course that's what you'd say. You only knew the best of her.'

'In the same way you only know the best of your mother.'

She wheeled away. 'The fact is neither of us knows what happened between them.'

That was true enough. He'd loved Frances, but she'd

been far from perfect. Still, she hadn't been imperfect enough to not be forgiven by her own flesh and blood.

Callie folded her arms. 'I have a feeling I'm not going to like Frances.'

He scowled back. What right did she think she had to judge her grandmother?

'That's right. Keep an open mind. Doesn't the fact that she's left you ridiculously wealthy mean anything?'

'I'm not keeping the inheritance if I don't like her!'

What?

'You signed the paperwork!'

'If I hadn't, what would've happened to the money, huh? Would it have gone to a cats' home?' She shook her head. 'I don't have anything against cats, but I can direct that money into better channels.'

'Like…?'

'Amnesty and the Red Cross…and that charity that distributes mosquito nets—it's a far from sexy one, but it's rated as getting great results.'

'The Against Malaria Foundation?'

'Yes! That one.'

They stared at each other, a little nonplussed. He shook himself. While Callie might've named three of his personal favourite charities, it was not what Frances had wanted her to do with the money.

'You'd really give the money away? The amount Frances has given you is life-changing.'

'Maybe I don't want my life changed.'

Something hard settled in the pit of his stomach. Frances would hate this outcome, and he was going to do everything he could to prevent it. By the time he was through with her, Callie Nicholls was going to acknowledge that her grandmother was a saint. Okay, maybe not a saint, but—

'Do *you* want it?' she asked.

He recoiled. 'No!'

She spread her hands as if that explained it all.

The reasons behind her initially tepid reaction to her inheritance hit him then. He'd thought she'd been hoping for more—for everything. He'd thought she'd been disappointed in the legacy Frances had left her. Instead, she'd been interested in Frances herself.

He dragged in a breath. While he already had his own twenty million dollars—and the rest—would he be able to just walk away from that sum, as Callie was threatening to do?

'The money doesn't have to be life-changing. It doesn't have to mean anything,' Callie said. 'Signing Mr Dunkley's paperwork will simply make accessing information easier. And frankly, Owen, that's all I'm interested in.'

'What kind of information are you after?' he asked.

While he might have been wrong about her returning Frances's letters, that didn't mean Callie Nicholls wasn't still trouble with a capital *T*.

CHAPTER THREE

EVER SINCE CALLIE had entered Frances's apartment, she'd grown more and more aware of Owen. Maybe it was because the apartment was an undeniably feminine space. Not in a pink and frilly way, but there were vases dotted about, waiting for flowers, scented candles lined the windowsills, and a plethora of cushions covered the sofas—more cushions than a man would ever put up with. Furthermore, the bookcase overflowed with novels—most of them romance and women's fiction.

The apartment was a feminine space, and Owen was undeniably masculine.

Or maybe it was the fact that she now understood why he'd been so angry, even though he'd tried to hide it. He'd thought she'd callously shunned a woman he'd cared about deeply. She didn't blame him for feeling the way he had.

What on earth had happened between her mother and Frances?

A chill chased across her scalp. Maybe she should leave the past where it was and not disturb it. Except...

She wanted to know, ached to learn all she could.

Here was a chance to discover where she came from, to find out if she had any other family and fill in all the blanks she'd been hungry to fill as a child. Here was a chance to *finally* get to the bottom of a mystery that had chafed at her for her entire childhood.

For as long as she could recall it had only been her and her mother. But they hadn't been alone in the world, as her mother had always claimed. She'd had a grandmother.

Her hands clenched and unclenched. She couldn't lie to herself. Her mother would have a good reason for keeping it from her. She suspected there'd be a price to pay for sating her curiosity. But also a prize to be won! And she couldn't forget that tracing her family tree would give her the chance to win an amazing job—one that would have Dominic grinding his teeth in envy and frustration.

She thrust out her jaw, resolve setting like concrete in her chest. Getting a new job, getting her life back on track and feeling in control again was her number one priority. She wasn't walking away now.

As for her inheritance and the money—she could make a decision about that at a later date.

She blinked herself back into the present to find herself staring at broad shoulders, lean hips and grey eyes that had turned as bleak as the mist her plane had flown through on its descent into New York.

In spite of what Frances had or hadn't done to Callie's mother, Owen had loved the older woman and he missed her. Her chest burned. She was intruding on that grief and taking away his sole source of comfort. She wanted to get to the bottom of this mystery, but not at the expense of other people.

'You know what, Owen? I really appreciate everything you've done, but I think I should find a nearby B&B. Maybe you'd be kind enough to suggest somewhere suitable and—?'

'What on earth are you talking about?'

She planted her hands on her hips. She stared at his strong thighs and her mouth went dry. *Don't stare.*

'And…uh…maybe you could hold the key for me until I'm ready to go through Frances's things?' His eyes narrowed, and she swallowed. 'Also, while I think of it, maybe there are a couple of Frances's things you'd like for yourself—for sentimental reasons. You should give it some thought and—'

'No, Callie.'

His face had cleared and he shook his head, his tone a strange combination of gentleness and implacability.

She blinked. 'I beg your pardon?'

'I'm not letting you do that.'

She puffed herself up, doing her best to feign offence. 'What do you mean *letting* me? It's *my* decision. The thing is, I'm sure I'll be much happier in a B&B.'

Beneath the soft wool of his jumper, his shoulders flexed. 'I know what you're doing, and I'd rather you didn't. Your grandmother would wish you to stay here. She certainly wouldn't want me coming here to wallow and be morose.'

'But—'

'It's time for me to move on. Now that you're in New York, I won't be coming here again without an invitation.'

'Fine! But you don't have to move on right this minute, you know? You can take your time and—'

He took her hands and squeezed, his smile warming his eyes. Her heart pressed hard against her lungs, making it difficult to catch her breath.

'Callie, I appreciate the thought. I really do. But it's totally unnecessary. This is just a place, and these are just things. I have my memories. That's enough.'

Her shoulders sagged, but some of the guilt lifted. 'If you're sure…?'

'Positive.'

He scanned her face and then nodded, as if satisfied with what he saw, but for a fraction of a moment his gaze lingered and the moment lengthened and slowed. She felt as if she were being tugged towards something unknown… something that promised richness and depth and meaning.

But then he blinked and dropped her hands, stepping back so quickly that instead of drifting along on a warm current she found herself having to plant her legs to keep her balance.

'Is there anything else I can do for you?'

His words emerged clipped and terse, and she automatically shook her head and pulled herself into straight lines.

'No, thank you. I don't need anything else.'

Drifting along on a warm current…? Had they been making eyes at each other? Surely not!

He glanced away, the muscles in his jaw bunching. 'I should take you out to dinner tonight…'

Except he didn't want to. That much was obvious. And she wasn't a damn charity case.

'No, you really shouldn't. Thanks for the thought, but no. It's been a hell of a day and jet-lag is catching up with me. I just want some quiet time to process everything that's happened.'

As she spoke, she moved towards the door, hoping he'd follow and leave. The absolute last thing she needed in her life was another complicated man.

'A quiet night in is exactly what the doctor ordered. I have your card. Why don't I give you a call sometime in the next couple of days and we can catch up over a coffee or something?'

Given his earlier desire to leave, he was now moving with studied reluctance. At the last moment he diverted to the kitchen, held up the apartment key, and set it on the counter.

She nodded her thanks. 'Like I said earlier, I appreciate all your help today.'

'It was nothing.'

They stood there for a moment in agonising awkwardness. What was the correct way to say goodbye to him? Kissing his cheek would be far too familiar, and yet shaking his hand felt too formal and wrong.

Eventually he nodded. 'Take care, Callie. If you need anything, don't hesitate to call.'

'Thanks.' She dug out a smile and offered a dumb little wave. 'See you.'

He turned and set off down the stairs and she closed the door, leaning back against it and blowing out a breath.

Even with their misunderstanding cleared up, she and Owen mixed like oil and water. It might be wise to spend as little time in each other's company as possible.

The sixteen-hour time difference between Sydney and New York didn't make for a restful night's sleep, even given Callie's exhaustion. At three a.m. she woke, ravenous enough for a three-course meal, but forced herself to remain where she was. She didn't fall back to sleep until after six, and then woke groggy and disoriented at nine.

A shower helped her feel halfway human, but before she could sally forth to find herself some breakfast and buy a phone charger a knock sounded on the door.

'Grocery delivery for Callie Nicholls.'

Owen had organised groceries for her? She'd been too beat to head out yesterday and find a store. She'd simply heated up a tin of soup she'd found in the pantry and made do with that.

The deliveryman set several bags on the kitchen bench and left again with a cheery 'Have a nice day.'

She made coffee and toast, and was flicking through the newspaper when a second knock sounded. Another delivery—one she had to sign for. When she opened the package she found a phone charger.

For all his reserve, there was no denying that Owen was taking his duty to assist her seriously. She pulled her phone out and started to call him—and then stopped.

He'd probably be at work by now. She texted him instead.

Thanks for groceries and charger. Dinner on me when new c card arrives.

He replied promptly with a thumbs-up emoji. She waited, but that was it.

'What more do you want?' she murmured, shaking her head and setting her phone on the charger, doing what she could to push thoughts of Owen from her mind.

Last night she'd decided to spend the day at the New York Public Library. She was a researcher, she wanted to find out all she could about her family, and where was the best place to research anything? A library.

She fell in love with the Fifth Avenue building the moment she stepped inside its grand marble foyer. And it was a love that only grew as she climbed the grand staircase to the third floor and the Rose Reading Room—a room the size of a football field, with arched casement windows that flooded the space with light, row upon row of antique wooden desks, and murals on the ceilings she stared at so long her neck started to ache.

She happily lost herself in its depths for several exhilarating hours.

Frances's family—*her* family—had links she could easily trace to sixteenth-century Europe. The family of Thomas—Frances's first husband and Callie's grandfather—was going to take a little more work, but she could already tell it wasn't going to be impossible.

She wasn't in the least interested in Frances's second husband Richard, as he had no blood ties to her, but it was impossible to avoid the headlines and photographs of them in the social pages—especially of their wedding and subsequent divorce. The wedding pictures showed a lavish affair, with the happy couple beaming at the camera. Frances looked absolutely ravishing, and much younger than her forty-six years of age. While Richard Bateman, twelve years her junior, was movie-star-handsome.

Callie fanned herself. *Way to go, Grandma.*

The divorce, though, had been an acrimonious affair.

From all accounts, Richard had been fundamentally inca-pable of fidelity. Callie winced at the far from flattering photo of Frances snapped only four years later, looking every inch her fifty years.

Maybe falling for jerks ran in the family.

Stop it. Her grandmother's first marriage sounded rock-solid. Everyone was allowed one or two romantic mistakes in their lifetime. Unfortunately, Frances's mistake had cost her several million dollars in the divorce settlement. At least Callie had only lost her job.

She stuck out her jaw. But not for long. Soon she'd have an even bigger, better, shinier job, and Dominic would be gnashing his teeth in envy.

And *that* would be perfect.

Returning to the apartment block mid-afternoon, she pushed open the door and a pint-sized dog, all cute honey-coloured fur, bolted from the foyer inside.

'Oh, no, no, no…little puppy, wait!' She pulled the door open wider, expecting to see the owner hurtling down the stairs after it, but nobody appeared.

'Don't even *think* about escaping,' she told the dog in her sternest teacher voice, not relishing the thought of chasing it all the way across New York.

But no sooner had the dog relieved itself against a nearby railing than it dashed back past her and inside again to race up the stairs. Oh, well. At least it was toilet-trained.

A door on the next landing opened, but the dog didn't pause. Callie called out a greeting as a woman emerged, but she only sent Callie a glare and returned inside, slam-ming the door behind her.

'Wow, so the locals are friendly, huh?' she muttered, set-ting off up the stairs. Still, this was a big city, not a country town where everyone said hello to each other.

She pulled up short when she reached the top floor and found the little dog sitting right outside Frances's door.

'Who do you belong to, little guy? Because you sure as heck don't live here?' There'd been no dog basket or water bowls in the apartment. He looked clean and well cared for, though, and he wore a collar. Someone in the complex must own him.

'You're lucky I like dogs,' she told him. 'Come in and have a drink and then we'll see if we can find where you live.'

It was time to introduce herself to the neighbours anyway.

He drank deeply from the bowl of water she set on the floor, and groaned in delight when she scratched his ears and rolled onto his back for a tummy rub.

'You're a little charmer...' she read the tag on his collar '... Barney.' There was no accompanying address or phone number.

She unpacked the few things she'd brought home with her from the library—a book and some printouts—before turning back to her four-legged visitor.

'C'mon, Barney. Let's see if we can find out who you belong to.'

She scooped him up from where he'd settled himself on the sofa. Rather than squirm or struggle, he licked her hand and happily settled in her arms.

'You're *so* good,' she cooed, tucking the key into the pocket of her jeans.

She decided to start on the fourth floor and work her way down. 'Hello,' she started brightly when a man answered the first door, 'I'm just wondering if this little guy belongs to you? I'm staying in the apartment upstairs and—'

'No, it doesn't.' The man glared at her. 'You got something against pets?'

'Of course not. It's just—'

But she found herself talking to the door that had been closed in her face.

'Did I hear Claude say you've got something against pets?' demanded the occupant of the other apartment on this floor.

'No, I—'

'Wanna kick me out 'cos I have a cat?'

She stilled. 'Do you know who I am?'

'We *all* know who you are.' And the woman shut the door in her face too.

She continued down to the next floor. The woman who hadn't returned her greeting earlier didn't even answer the door, though Callie could've sworn she was at home. She turned to find the door of the apartment opposite open, and a man glaring at her.

'Not my dog,' he growled.

'How did you—?'

'Heard you upstairs.'

Were the walls that thin around here?

'You coming down here to tell me you're increasing the rent?'

She moistened dry lips. 'Nope.'

'You expect me to believe that?'

Her spine stiffened. 'Yes.'

'Well, I don't. And don't go disturbing Jilly in Number One. She works nights and needs her rest.'

'Right. Thank you. I—' She rolled her eyes. 'And I'm talking to another door.'

By the time she reached the basement apartment she was feeling ragged. She raised her hand and knocked, not sure if she hoped to find the resident at home or not. A firm tread sounded.

She pushed her shoulders back. No matter how glaring and bad-tempered this person might be, she would not turn tail and run. She lifted her chin, determined to give as good as she got.

The door opened, she hiked up her gaze…and her jaw dropped.

'Owen!'

Callie Nicholls stood on his doorstep, and at the sight of her something low down in Owen's gut sprang to life. He tried to stamp it out, exterminate it. For pity's sake, if he concentrated hard enough he *would* conquer the inconvenient heat flooding his veins. He just had to try harder.

A glance at her face, though, and all that was forgotten. The corners of her mouth drooped, her shoulders were hunched up towards her ears, and tiny lines fanned out from her eyes. She looked dragged down, worn thin…exhausted.

'What's up?'

'You really don't want to know…' The bitter edge to her words made him stiffen. 'But maybe you can answer a few questions for me.'

'Right, hit me with them.' He'd meant the words to sound rallying, encouraging. Instead they'd emerged clipped—like a command—making him wince internally.

Get a new hotel.

Treat your grandmother with respect.

Tell me your questions.

Way to woo a girl, Owen.

Not that he had any interest in wooing this girl. He had no interest in wooing *any* girl. He might find her attractive, but he wasn't making a play for her.

She stuck out a hip and his mouth dried.

'One: why does everyone in this building hate me?'

Ah.

'Two: does this dog belong to you?'

He glanced at the little dog cradled in her arms, but before he could answer she powered on.

'Three: why didn't you tell me you lived in the basement apartment of the block I've inherited? What's the big secret?'

It took all his strength not to fidget.

'And four,' she continued after a short pause, 'are you going to invite me in?'

In answer to her last question he pushed the door open wider and waved her in. 'But before you put the dog down, let me close my office door.'

His office was the first room off the hallway that led to the rest of the apartment, and the door stood wide open. He'd been working when she'd knocked.

Her eyes widened when she glanced past him and caught sight of his computer equipment. 'You have some fancy-schmancy computer gear there, Owen.' She ruffled the dog's ears. 'And we sure as heck don't want you getting in there and causing havoc, Barney.'

'Most of the equipment belongs to my company.'

'The company you work for?'

'Yep.'

He omitted the salient fact that he owned the company. He wasn't ready to trust her. He tried telling himself that who he was and what he did was no concern of hers, but it didn't ring true. Whatever. It had no bearing on their current conversation.

'You can put Barney down now. It should be safe.'

Her lips twitched. 'Fingers crossed—but I refuse to give any guarantees. Barney and I aren't all that well acquainted yet.'

They followed the little dog as he trotted down the hallway and into the open-plan living room.

'Oh!' Callie pulled up short when she saw it. 'I thought it'd be dark and poky down here, but it's…'

'Not?' he finished for her, moving towards the fridge.

'It's amazing.'

It was. Light flooded into the room from the French

doors that led outside to a small private courtyard. The living room walls were painted a warm cream, and the pale furniture reflected back the light, making the room appear airy and spacious. He could afford something much grander these days, but he didn't want grander. Not at the moment.

'Beer?' he said.

'Beer?'

She swung from surveying a picture on his wall, her eyes widening and her lips curving in a way that chased away all the shadows.

Don't focus on the lips.

'Yes, please!'

Her enthusiasm made him grin. 'I forgot. Aussies and beer go hand in hand, don't they? Or is that an outdated cliché?'

'Nope, it's pretty much a national standard. Trying American beer is on my list of must-dos while I'm here.'

'If it's not up to scratch I can point you towards a couple of local liquor stores that probably stock Australian beer.'

She stared at him, and then she smiled, and for a moment the world tilted.

'That's kind of you.' She hiked herself up to sit on one of the stools at his breakfast bar.

He handed her a beer. And then remembered his manners. 'Glass?'

She shook her head, glancing back behind her to see the dog lay sprawled in a patch of sun, completely at ease. 'This little guy has a habit of making himself at home wherever he is. So...?'

She turned back, eyebrows raised. He ordered himself not to stare.

'How about I answer your questions in reverse order?' he said.

She sipped her beer, her eyes not leaving his.

He didn't move to take the stool beside her, but remained

leaning back against the kitchen bench, the breakfast bar between them. Cool, casual, unruffled—those were the things he needed to be.

'First up—yes, I am going to invite you in.'

A current of electricity surged through him when her lips twitched.

'Thank you. I'm honoured.'

'I didn't mention the fact that I live in the same building as Frances because it slipped my mind. And it didn't seem important. I moved back into the block eight months ago, but it's only a temporary measure.'

She set her beer down carefully. 'You didn't tell me you live down here because you don't trust me. That made sense when you thought I'd been mean to someone you loved, but it's still the case now...' She stared at him. 'I suppose that means your natural default position is suspicious?'

He straightened. 'No, it's not. I...'

The denial petered out and he forced himself back into an attitude of casual slouchiness. The little dog trotted over to sit at his feet, staring up at him. He welcomed the change of focus.

'You thirsty, little guy?'

He set a bowl of water down for the dog, but Barney rolled onto his back instead, begging for a tummy rub. With a low laugh, Owen obliged before forcing himself upright again.

'It never used to be my default position,' he made himself say. Before Fiona it hadn't been. But now...

'So I shouldn't take it personally?'

'You shouldn't take it personally,' he agreed.

They stared at each other, neither moving, and in that stillness something changed—stirred and unfurled, charging the air. A fist reached into his chest and gently but inexorably squeezed the breath from his body. Panic fluttered at the edges of his consciousness and he had to wrench his gaze away before he did something stupid. Like walk across and kiss her.

What the hell...?

His heart pounded and Callie's dazed expression, the way her fingers tightened about her beer, the way her jaw tightened, told him she'd recognised what he hadn't been able to disguise—that he found her attractive...that he wanted her.

She took a long pull on her drink, looking everywhere but at him. Had he made her feel uncomfortable? Or—worse—unsafe?

He didn't want her feeling unsafe around him.

'Sometimes you remind me of Frances.' The words dropped into the silence that surrounded them. 'And it catches me off guard.'

It was the truth, but it wasn't what that moment had been about. Still, it would provide him with some kind of excuse, at least. And hopefully help her feel at ease again.

She froze—head tilted back, bottle of beer to her lips. Nothing moved except her eyes as they returned to his. Eventually she lowered the bottle, but she didn't speak.

'It's in the way you raise your eyebrows. Especially when you quirk just one of them.' He huffed out a laugh. 'Exactly like you're doing now.'

She lifted a hand to her eyebrow, as if committing the mannerism to memory.

'You have a rather precise way of moving your hands... And your chin,' he added with a frown, the resemblance only striking him now, 'is the same shape as Frances's.'

'It's the same shape as my mother's too.'

She traced it with her fingers and he tried not to imagine following the action with his own hand, then tilting it so he could lower his mouth over hers and—

He pushed away from the bench. At her questioning glance he gestured across the room. 'The sofa's more comfortable.' He needed to sit.

His sofa was a deep, L-shaped affair, but before he could plant himself in the far corner the little dog had beaten him to it.

'That's a little bold, Barney,' she scolded, scooting across to lift him onto her lap. 'Owen might not want you sitting on his sofa.'

Owen took the seat furthest away, aware now of her fragrance. She smelled like spring flowers. Or maybe that was because his courtyard was filled with a profusion of the spring blooms his mother had planted.

'I don't mind him being on the sofa.'

She glanced around and huffed out a sigh. 'But he's not yours, is he?'

It was more of a statement than a question, and things inside him pulled tight. He was a dog person. What was it about his apartment that gave her the idea he wasn't?

'No dog bed or food bowls or dog toys,' she continued, and his shoulders loosened. 'You wouldn't happen to know who he belongs to, by any chance?'

He shook his head. 'What made you think I would?'

She told him how she and Barney had become acquainted.

'He must be local,' he agreed, curbing the temptation to reach over and fondle the dog's ears. It would bring him too close to Callie. 'He looks well cared for.'

She nodded.

'Right.' He stood. 'Lost dogs are usually found within the first hour of going missing. I suggest we walk the nearby streets to see if anyone is searching for him.'

'Excellent plan!'

They returned to his apartment an hour and a half later, none the wiser and with Barney still trotting obediently on the length of cord Owen had dug out of the bottom of a drawer. They flopped down onto his sofa, nursing bottles of water.

'He can stay with me until I find his owner.' Callie glanced at Barney and then at Owen. 'I get the feeling you're a dog person too?' He nodded, and her eyes lit up. 'You work from home, right?'

'What makes you say that?'

These days he volunteered as little information about himself as possible. He'd been too trusting, too open, with Fiona, and it wasn't a mistake he meant to repeat.

'Your office is huge. So I just thought…' She shrugged. 'I figured it meant you worked from home sometimes.'

'Sometimes I do.'

He refused to meet her eyes. He had to go into the office occasionally. When he had meetings with clients, or his team of programmers, but it was rare. He left the day-to-day running of the company in the capable hands of his office manager. Ninety-five per cent of his work he did in the comfort of his own home.

'Then we can share custody of Barney, if you like. I'm doing some research at the New York Public Library. It'd be great if I could leave him with you for a few hours each day when I do that.'

'Sure, why not?'

Lissy had been on to him for ages to get a dog. Barney would provide the perfect trial run. Maybe he could use Barney as an enticement to get Lissy to come and stay one weekend soon…

He reached across and tugged gently on Barney's ear. 'How'd you feel about that, Barney Boy? We can have some guy time. You can kick back over a bowl of kibble while I slave over a hot computer.'

He eased back, doing his best to ignore the scent of spring and the impulsive restlessness it sent surging through his veins. So, the New York Public Library…? What was she researching?

He watched as Callie rubbed the little dog's neck and

shoulders, and laughed when Barney groaned his delight, kicking his back legs.

'It might be worth putting some posters up around the area to help track down his owner. I could take Barney's picture, make a poster, run a few copies off… What do you think?'

'That's a great idea. Someone has to be fretting about him, and we ought to spread the word. First thing tomorrow I'll ring around the local vets. They might know who he is.'

Her face grew serious again and the silence stretched, making Owen's nape prickle.

'You do know you still haven't answered the first of my earlier questions?'

He scratched a hand over his face.

'Why do all the residents here hate me, Owen?'

'They don't hate you. They're just worried. Worried you're going to evict them or hike up their rents and force them out.'

'I see.'

She folded her arms and Barney leapt off her lap to pad over to the warm patch of sun outside, where he proceeded to stretch out as if on a minibreak at Waikiki Beach.

'Really strategic move, being rude to me, though… Right? That's the perfect plan to have me warming to everyone and feeling sympathetic and benevolent.'

He bit back something rude and succinct. How did he explain the motley crew that made up the residents of this apartment block?

'Joan in Number Six is a victim of domestic violence. Her now ex-husband is in prison for assaulting her. He contravened a restraining order—wasn't supposed to be within a hundred yards of her.'

She flinched.

'Stuart in Number Four turned to drugs and alcohol as a teenager, due to childhood sexual abuse. He's clean now, but it's a constant struggle for him. He works part-time and is on a disability pension. He sees a therapist several times a week.'

She swallowed.

'Ana from Number Three—her parents were illegal immigrants. When her father was extradited back to Ecuador he was murdered. She and her mother, who is nearly crippled with arthritis, are fighting to stay in the country.'

'Okay, okay...' She waved her hands in front of her face. 'I get it. Everyone here has had a tough time.' She pulled in a breath. 'Change—any kind of change—will be frightening for them.'

'They have zero expectation of receiving kindness from strangers, Callie. It's not what they've been taught to anticipate.'

Behind the startling blue of her eyes, he could see her mind turning over.

'Frances took each of them in?'

'Yes.'

'She offered them a safe place and cheap rent, just like she did for your mother?'

His gut twisted. Now came the moment of truth. If Callie really was a gold-digger she'd hike up the rents. She could get ten times what everyone here was paying. She could price them out and force them out.

His back molars ground together. He wouldn't let that happen. If he had to, he'd subsidise the tenants' rents. Not that he had any intention of telling her that. The people here had been through enough for one lifetime. Frances had wanted to give them a safe place to shelter and rebuild their lives. He'd continue that legacy for as long as he could.

'I've no intention of changing things for the foreseeable future, Owen.'

His heart hammered against his ribs. 'What *are* your plans for the foreseeable future?'

CHAPTER FOUR

'Wow, YOU MUST be really good at your job!' Callie couldn't help but be impressed with all the high-end equipment in Owen's home office.

'Or just a tech nerd.' He didn't glance up from manipulating an image of Barney on the screen for the promised poster.

'You said you create apps?' At his nod, she added, 'Would I be familiar with anything you've worked on?'

His gaze remained glued to his screen, but he named a couple of apps that had her eyebrows shooting up towards her hairline.

'Wow! If you worked on those then no wonder you have an office at home like this.'

'What do you mean?' He swung around, his tone clipped.

She blinked. 'I just meant it's clear your company will do whatever it can to keep you happy...so you'll keep working for them.'

With a curt nod he turned back to the computer.

She soldiered on past the awkwardness. 'I guess the beauty of working from home is you can ditch the power suits and work in jeans and a tee.' Although Owen didn't strike her as a power suit kind of guy... 'Or even your PJs, if you want.' Though Owen might be one of those guys who wore nothing at all to bed.

Her cheeks grew suddenly hot and her palms clammy.

His lips twisted. 'I bet you like a guy in a power suit.'

There was an edge to the question that raised her hackles. 'Mmm, you bet... What woman doesn't, right? I mean it's *dreamy*.'

She wondered if she'd overdone it, but he swung back

to his computer with a scowl. 'The commute is *mmm, dreamy* too.'

There was clearly something about her that made him want to snipe at her. And vice versa. Grief on his part, maybe? And the shock of being thrust into this seemingly alternative reality on hers? This ruffling and needling and poking at each other should feel stressful, fraught…nerve-racking. It didn't, though. It felt enlivening…*energising.*

For a moment earlier she'd even thought Owen had wanted to kiss her. It had sent a thrill of something gloriously reckless powering through her veins and—

Don't even go there.

She wasn't getting involved with anyone at the moment. She wasn't in the right frame of mind to start a relationship, so what was the point?

Fun? The word had some of the hardness inside her wanting to soften and thaw, but she refused to let it. That kind of fun would distract her from working on the things that really mattered—work and stability. The distraction might look tempting, but it wasn't worth it. Not in the long run.

She tossed her head and forced herself back to the conversation. 'The downside of working from home, of course, is not having workmates,' she said.

She missed her work colleagues. Not Dominic and the Head of Faculty—she didn't miss them one little bit. But the rest of the staff in the history department had been a fun bunch. They'd welcomed her, advised her, and on occasion challenged her. They'd taught her so much about becoming an efficient researcher and a good teacher. She missed them. She missed her students too. She'd hate to work from home like Owen did.

She glanced down to find cool grey eyes assessing her. He leaned back in his chair, the poster evidently forgotten. 'You miss the people you work with, Callie? I'm guessing you're not a computer nerd. What is it that you do?'

'Did,' she corrected. 'Past tense. I was a junior history lecturer at a university back home.'

'You were fired?'

'Nothing so dramatic. I was *"let go"*.' She made air quotes. 'My contract wasn't renewed.'

His eyes gentled. 'Downsizing?'

'The powers that be are always trying to downsize the arts.' Not that she'd really been a victim of downsizing. She'd been a victim of sexism and an old-style boys' club mentality. It wasn't a mistake she'd make again.

She glanced around his office. 'It must be nice to be so good at something and to be valued for it. I envy you.'

'I'm sure you were very good at what you did.'

She'd thought so too. She'd thought she was safe. 'Maybe if I'd been better at it I wouldn't have been *let go*.'

'We both know that workplace politics comprise so much more than a worker's individual worth, Callie.'

'Truer words…' she quipped, refusing to dwell on her sense of injury and the stinging injustice of it all. She'd keep her eyes firmly fixed on the main prize. 'Currently I'm between jobs, but there are prospects on the horizon—' *good prospects* '—and I'm quite sure work colleagues will feature in my future.'

'Good for you.'

'What about you? Don't you miss having work colleagues?' she asked as he turned back to the screen. 'Though I suppose you're an island complete unto himself.'

His lips twitched, and she had the oddest feeling she could stare at those lips all day.

'I might not go into an office on a daily basis, but I'm not a hermit. I have online meetings, brainstorming sessions with other programmers. And outside of work this apartment block is a little community in itself.'

One she was currently excluded from. Being excluded sucked. She needed to do something to change that.

'I also see my family and friends regularly,' he said.

She held up a piece of sporting memorabilia—a pewter man swinging some kind of bat mounted on a shiny walnut base. 'And who do you attend ballgames with?'

'Don't drop that—it's a limited edition. Not cheap.'

She very carefully placed it back on its shelf. 'What sort of ballgame…?'

'Baseball. And the fact you had to ask tells me you know nothing about ballgames.'

'Not a thing.' And, strangely enough, her life didn't feel the poorer for it.

'And sometimes,' he continued, 'when I'm wrestling with the logic of a particularly difficult piece of code, I'll work at a nearby coffee house.'

She clapped her hands beneath her chin. 'Like the one in *Friends*?'

He laughed. 'It looks nothing like the one in *Friends*. It's larger…more beaten up…no sofas.'

'It sounds kinda cool.'

'It is. You'd probably like it. Lots of guys in high-powered suits.'

'Oh, I'm sold! Address, please? I'll make sure to drop by.'

His hand stilled on the keyboard. Above the photo of Barney that was centred on the page he'd written *Found* and beneath that he'd written *Answers to the name of Barn*.

'You want to meet someone while you're here?' he asked.

A temporary fling with a like-minded guy would be the perfect way to drive Dominic from her mind and her heart once and for all—that and the job. Her heart pounded up into her throat. *The job*… She *had* to convince the producers of that show that she was the perfect candidate.

She released her breath and shook her head. 'I can't afford the distraction of a fling at the moment.' She pointed to his screen. 'It's Barney. With an *E-Y. B-A-R-N-E-Y.*'

He typed *E-Y.* 'Distraction from what?'

She couldn't work out if he was grilling her or if he was genuinely interested. 'When I told you I didn't know what my plans were, I meant about my inheritance and this building.' Now that she knew he lived here and worked from here, his concern made more sense. 'But I have a job plan I'm working on.'

He spun around on his chair. 'Which is…?'

She gestured to his spare chair, silently asking if she could sit in it.

'Knock yourself out.' He grabbed the pile of files on it and set them on his desk.

'Have you heard of the TV programme *Mystery Family Trees*? It's a British TV series that's proved so popular in the UK they've made an Australian version too.'

His brow creased. 'The show where they trace a celebrity's genealogy?'

'That's the one. Well, they're now in the process of putting a team together to make an American version of the show.'

'Uh-huh…'

'And I'm an historian.' She spread her hands and kinked an eyebrow. 'See where I'm going with this?'

'That mouth of yours is going to get you into trouble one day.'

But one corner of his own mouth lifted as he said it, and then his gaze lowered to her lips and time seemed to stand still. The murmur of a sighing breeze brushed through her, transporting her somewhere warm and sultry, like a tropical beach. Doors firmly shut inside her cracked open a fraction and—

Owen snapped away and swung back to his computer. She blinked, the warmth inside her icing over as the present crashed back.

Keep talking. Don't let the silence stretch. Pretend nothing happened.

Nothing *had* happened. And nothing was *going* to happen.

'So, my plan is to put together a little video of me uncovering my own family tree to send in with my application.'

She was sure she didn't imagine him pushing several inches away on the wheels of his office chair before turning back towards her. The expression in his eyes, though, was alive with interest, and she could almost see him joining the dots.

'So the discovery of your grandmother…?'

'Has opened heretofore unknown doors.'

'And the research you've been doing at the New York Public Library…?'

'Has been to trace my family history. Which, I have to say, has been pretty straightforward. I've been able to go back five generations. I've hunted out locations I can visit to add colour to my personal documentary. And there's the possibility of a skeleton in the closet, with a younger son mysteriously missing in the eighteen-hundreds—"missing" as in I've not been able to find any further records of him yet. I suspect the family shipped him off somewhere to hush up some scandal. I also suspect, given enough time, I can get to the bottom of it.'

He stared at her. 'That's a good plan. Actually…it's inspired. It should land you the job for sure.'

She wrinkled her nose. 'Except my area of expertise is Australian history, rather than personal or family history. But research is research, right? Regardless of the topic, the skill-set is the same.'

'I'd have thought so—especially if you can showcase those skills in action.'

She slumped. 'The thing is…'

He leaned towards her. 'What's the thing?'

'While I might be finding it easy enough to trace my mother's side of the family…'

'Yes?'

The grey of his eyes looked like smoke—all misty and mysterious like a Scottish moor she'd like to explore.

'Callie?'

She snapped back. 'The problem is I've absolutely no idea who my father might be.'

'What, nothing?'

'*Nichts. Nada.* Nothing. My mother refuses to talk about him, and his name isn't on my birth certificate. Something really bad must've gone down.'

'But this is your *father*. Everyone has the right to know who their father is.'

'You think so?'

She was less convinced. It didn't stop her from aching to know where she had come from, though. She hitched up her chin. Besides, there was the job to consider. She was determined to do everything in her power to win it.

'Of course they do. Even if it's just to access a medical history. That stuff can be important.'

'But what if he's violent—a criminal? What if he beat my mother up and raped her? I can't see how me knowing that will help anyone.'

He rubbed a hand over his face.

'And even if he didn't...' things inside her hardened '... I just know he has to be a nasty piece of work. What I do know is she loved him.' The kind of heartbreak her mother had evidently suffered only came from the deepest love...and the deepest betrayal. 'And, as I was born only four months after my mother emigrated to Australia, I'm thinking it's a fairly safe bet that he's American.'

Owen nodded.

'I'm guessing that when she told him she was pregnant he wanted nothing to do with her or a baby.' But of course she had no proof of that.

'Or perhaps she loved him so much she left to protect him from a scandal? Maybe he was someone important?'

'Or already married.' She surveyed him for a moment. 'You said you and Frances liked to watch *Law and Order*. Does that mean you enjoy a good mystery?'

'I must do. I work with computer code. It's a lot like trying to put the pieces of a jigsaw puzzle together.' He raised an eyebrow. 'Does your mother know what you're trying to do?'

'I haven't said as much, but... She knows me. She knows I'll dig. I haven't told her about the job yet, or how I plan to win it.'

He rested his elbows on his knees, his eyes gentling. 'Callie, don't you think if you told her how important this job is to you she'd tell you the truth?'

He smelled like warm cotton and talcum powder, and something homemade baking in the oven.

'You've been watching too many sappy rom-coms,' she teased, to hide the way her pulse had quickened.

Breathing him in felt nourishing in a way the tin of soup she'd heated up for her dinner last night hadn't. She battled a bolt of pure temptation. It would be so easy to lean across and kiss him.

She shot to her feet to pace around his office, in an attempt to distract herself from the shape of a mouth she had a feeling would now figure prominently in her dreams.

'You don't want to distress your mother?' he asked.

'She's just become engaged.' She glanced over her shoulder to smile at him. 'I'm so pleased for her. I've never seen her so happy.' She traced a finger along a square glass case that held a signed ball—a baseball, she supposed. 'You really like these Mets, huh?'

'More than life itself.' He paused. 'And your mother?'

She was going to be facetious and say she was pretty sure her mother wasn't a Mets fan, but she bit it back and returned to her seat instead. 'This is the first time I've seen her truly happy in a romantic relationship.'

Understanding dawned in his eyes. 'And you don't want to mar that by bringing up the past?'

'Correctamundo,' she said, doing her best Fonz impression. 'It's cool. I'll just work it out for myself. In fact I *want* to work it out myself. Only then will I be able to prove my worth and convince the producers of *Mystery Family Trees* to hire me.'

'Except you don't have a single lead.'

'You think? I'd place all my twenty million dollars on a bet that Frances knew what happened. I'm betting that's what they fell out about. And I'm guessing Frances wished she'd given my mother more support and has regretted not doing so ever since. Hence the letters.'

'It's a possibility... But Frances wasn't a prude or a stickler. She wouldn't have cared about her daughter becoming a single mother.' He glanced up. 'What's your plan?'

'To read Frances's letters and see if she makes any mention of it, or see if there's some clue in them. Other than that... She must have an address book somewhere. I could ring her friends...tell them who I am. Maybe they'll agree to meet with me. Someone will know what happened back then. They always do.'

He stared.

She stifled the urge to roll her shoulders. 'What?'

'You're going to all this trouble for a job?'

'It's a good job.' She hitched her chin at his office. 'This looks like a good job too—seems to me you're getting to call a lot of your own shots. What lengths would you go to to keep it?'

He huffed out a laugh, as if acknowledging the hit. 'Okay... The thing is, Frances didn't have many friends. If she did before I knew her, she'd lost touch with them by the time my mother and I moved here.'

A four-year-old kid going through the kind of upheaval Owen had been would've noticed everything. He would've kept watch and noted every person who entered the building, working out who belonged and who didn't. He'd have kept watch for the father who scared him. Her heart burned at all he must've gone through.

'I do know the few people she did keep in touch with, though. And I remember the names of those she occasionally talked about from the good old days.'

He did…?

He leaned back slightly. 'I'll make a deal with you.'

'What kind of deal?'

'I'll do whatever I can to help you find out who your father is…'

Her heart leapt. He was smart. He knew how to put a puzzle together *and* he had inside information. She'd be crazy to refuse his help.

'And in return?'

'If you decide you're going to donate your inheritance to charity…'

'Yes?'

'Will you sell the apartment block to me first, rather than donating the building lock, stock and barrel?'

She stared. 'You can afford to buy it?' Just exactly how good was this job of his?

In the next moment she dismissed the thought. If he had that kind of money he wouldn't be living in a basement apartment—not even one as nice as this.

His eyes had turned opaque. 'There's a co-op I know that would be interested in taking it and its current residents over.'

A charity? It was funny… Yesterday she wouldn't have thought he was the kind of man to concern himself with the down and out. Today she could see how wrong she'd been.

'I'm not asking for a discount—you'd be offered the market value.'

It was a no-brainer. 'You have yourself a deal.'

'Or,' he continued, 'if you decide to keep your inheritance but sell the building—'

'You'll have first dibs.'

'Thank you.'

They shook on it.

'A party!' She leapt to her feet as the inspiration occurred to her. 'That's what I'll do. I'll throw a party for everyone. A block party. And then they'll all like me. Just you wait and see.'

'So what *is* she like?'

Owen glanced at his mother as they passed into Washington Square Park through the western entrance. Sixteen-year-old Lissy trailed along behind, dragging her feet and looking bored in the way that only a teenager could.

'She seems nice enough.' They stopped to watch a game of chess in action. White Knight moved to C4 and he could see at a glance how he could win the game in three moves if he were playing black.

'And all the letters Frances sent?'

They walked on. A squirrel scampered across the grass, all twitchy motion, and he started to feel twitchy too, though he had no idea why. 'It appears she knew nothing about them. It was Donna who intercepted and returned them all.'

'That makes a strange kind of sense.'

It did? He stared at her before swinging around to find Lissy had fallen even further behind and had started talking to some guy who was *way* too old for her. And who was eyeing her up in her short, short skirt like a Rottweiler would a piece of porterhouse.

He slammed to a halt. 'Lissy!'

With an eye-roll, she gave the guy a wave before continuing towards them. 'Spoilsport,' she muttered, drawing up on his other side. And then she rolled her eyes. 'Relax... I know him, okay?'

'How?' he demanded, and winced. He didn't mean to sound so damn censorious, and he could've kicked himself when her face closed up and she didn't bother answering. 'Look, Lissy, I'm sorry. It's just—'

But he was talking to thin air. Lissy had hurried on towards a small group of girls.

His mother shook her head. 'When are you going to learn, Owen?'

The mild reprimand made him feel even smaller. But, *damn*, his little half-sister had turned into a ball of sarcastic prickliness over the last year. The sunny-natured kid who'd once adored him was long gone. She worried the heck out of him. She was boy-mad, and the clothes she wore were designed to attract the attention of every male in a ten-mile radius.

He ground his teeth together. The kind of attention from the kind of guy that had a brother's every protective hackle rising.

They were moving in the direction of the fountain in the middle of the park, with the familiar shape of the Washington Square Arch up ahead on their left, when he saw Callie and Barney seated on the grass with three teenage girls around the same age as Lissy. He halted and stared.

'Owen, if I didn't know you better I'd say you were ogling that young woman.'

He snapped to attention, shook himself. 'That's her. That's Callie Nicholls.'

'It appears she's made some friends.'

When? How? When did she have the time...?

Lissy ambled back, but the barely suppressed excitement in her eyes belied her affected nonchalance. She surreptitiously pointed to one of the girls in Callie's circle. 'That's Angelina Michaels.'

She said it in a reverent tone that clued Owen in that Angelina was *somebody*. He racked his brain. 'Who is she again?' But then he remembered. 'The basketball star at your school?' From memory, she was a year ahead of Lissy.

'She's a goddess. You should see her play. Amazing!'

A smile built through him. Maybe this was his chance to redeem himself a little in her eyes. 'Would you like to meet her?'

She shushed him. 'We can't just go over there!'

'What if I can swing a casual introduction because I know the person she's talking to?'

Lissy stared, a gleam starting up in the depths of her eyes. 'Then I might, *perhaps*, forgive you for being such a bossy bore so far today.'

His jaw dropped. 'Bossy bore?'

'The moment you clapped eyes on my skirt this morning you started being as prissy and snippy as an ancient aunt in one of those Dickens or Austen books I have to read for school.'

'If you had more sense I wouldn't have—'

'I'd like to meet her.'

His mother's voice broke through their bickering, reminding Owen that he was supposed to be the older and wiser sibling. It was just that he worried so much for Lissy—was worried she'd fall in with the wrong crowd, worried that some guy would treat her the way his father had treated his mother. He'd do everything he could to protect her from that.

It was Barney who saw them first, giving a clear, resounding bark—he had a big bark for such a little dog—and straining on his lead towards Owen. Callie glanced around, her lips curving into her trademark smile when she saw him. Jumping to her feet, she shook both his mother and

Lissy's hands when he introduced them, before introducing her own trio of… Acquaintances? Friends?

He glanced at the girls and gestured to the books and laptops. 'What are you all up to?'

'Callie's helping us study for our Math final,' one of the girls said.

He couldn't hide his surprise. 'But Callie's a History major, not Math.'

'They're not mutually exclusive,' she teased. 'I was probably better at Math than I was at History. I just enjoyed History more.' Her face lit up. 'Hey, you might be able to help. Micah is having some trouble with her computer science elective and it's beyond my skill-set.'

Before he knew what he was about, Owen found himself sitting on the grass tutoring Micah while Callie skilfully steered the others into a discussion about basketball when Lissy mentioned her admiration for Angelina's game. Then she smiled at his mother and led her to a nearby bench. 'I was hoping I'd get a chance to meet you and maybe chat a bit about Frances, Mrs O'Sullivan.'

'You must call me Margaret.'

And that was all he heard. But as he took in Lissy's glowing face when Angelina invited her to shoot some hoops with her one afternoon the following week, and heard his mother laugh at something Callie said, he found he didn't mind sitting in the spring sunshine explaining the vagaries of the Math that Micah was struggling with. They were a nice bunch, and he enjoyed the good-natured way they teased each other, and the way they included Lissy in both their discussions and their teasing.

He'd have been happy to sit there for another hour, except Micah gave a start as she glanced at her watch. '*Gah!* I have to go or I'll be late for my shift at Burger Co.'

Angelina groaned. 'I promised Mom I'd babysit tonight. If I don't get home soon it'll be panic stations.'

The three girls said their goodbyes and were soon gone.

'That was awesome,' Lissy breathed as they joined their mother and Callie. 'Angelina is the best point guard our school has had in ten years.'

Callie smiled. 'They're a fun bunch.'

Owen stared at her. 'How did you meet them?'

When the muscles in Callie's jaw tightened, Lissy rolled her eyes and his mother shook her head.

He grimaced. 'Sorry, I didn't mean that to sound so…'

Lissy folded her arms. 'Bossy?'

He resisted the urge to run a finger around the collar of his sweater. 'Like I was giving you the third degree.'

Callie glanced at Lissy. 'You get this a lot?'

'All. The. Time.'

Callie raised an eyebrow at him. 'It's a bit much, isn't it?'

A scowl built through him, but before he could reply his mother spoke. 'We're having dinner with Owen this evening. We'd love it if you could join us, Callie.'

What on earth…?

Callie glanced at him, as if she sensed he might be feeling less than hospitable. He checked himself internally and discovered he wasn't as averse to the idea as he probably should be.

He huffed out a laugh and shook his head. 'We would,' he confirmed.

'Then I'd love to.'

Her smile seemed to make things inside him click into place—which made no sense. *She* made no sense. He frowned. Actually, now that he thought about it, could he retract the dinner invitation?

The women all seemed completely at home with each other, strolling along and chatting, and Lissy was utterly delighted to be handed Barney's lead. He felt oddly left out. Eventually they turned back the way they'd come, and it was only as they drew abreast of the collection of chess tables that the idea hit him.

'Do you play, Callie?' He wanted to trounce her. At just one thing. He knew the impulse was childish, but he couldn't contain it.

'I do.' Blue eyes assessed him. 'And I'm pretty good.'

'So am I.'

She turned to face him fully. 'Are you challenging me to a game?'

He wanted to wipe the floor with her—figuratively speaking—and get a sense of control back. He glanced at his mom and Lissy.

'It's too early to start preparing dinner yet,' his mom said. 'I'm happy to sit here in the park in this lovely sun.'

'Don't do it,' Lissy said to Callie. 'He's really good.'

'So am I, baby doll,' Callie said, affecting a gangster stance and pretending to straighten her non-existent collar.

Lissy giggled and slipped an arm through Callie's, apparently BFFs.

Callie played white. He was black.

And she whooped his butt.

And to his shock he found that he didn't mind at all.

'Where did you learn to play like that?'

'My mum is obsessed with the game. It's a rare occasion that I can beat her.'

Owen's stomach burned. Had Frances taught him to play because the game had reminded her of her daughter?

Callie swung to Lissy, the glossy auburn highlights in her hair gleaming in the sun. 'Did you hear I had all of my things stolen?'

Lissy's mouth dropped open. 'All of your clothes too?' She whimpered at Callie's nod. 'I'd have bawled my eyes out.'

Had Callie wanted to cry? He squirmed as he recalled

what he'd thought about her...how mistaken he'd been. He should've been more sympathetic, kinder...gentler.

'Your brother was great—he had some essentials delivered and took care of everything. I was so grateful.'

She sent him a smile that made him feel like a million dollars.

'But I still need to buy some clothes. Are there any stores around here you can recommend? I've no idea, and—'

'I could go shopping with you!' Lissy's face lit up. 'Tomorrow? It'd be fun.' She grinned at her brother. 'Owen would let me crash for the night. I mean you've been nagging me to stay for, like, for *ever*, right?'

She was volunteering to stay *the whole night*? He did his best not to sound too eager. 'Sure.'

'Is it okay, Mom?'

'Sure, honey—but only if it's okay with Callie. She might have plans.'

'No plans.' Callie nudged Lissy's shoulder. 'I'd love it.'

He wanted to hug her for the grin she sent his little sister.

'And maybe we could all watch a movie after dinner,' Lissy added.

'Sounds like fun,' Callie agreed.

Both of them turned to him and he raised his hands in surrender. 'Any chance I get to choose the movie?'

'None at all,' Lissy said, with a cheerfulness that warmed him all the way through.

'Fine...' he pretended to grumble. But the plan sounded absolutely perfect.

CHAPTER FIVE

SEEING OWEN WITH his family was like viewing him through an entirely new lens. He'd lost that almost unconscious edge he had whenever he was around her. He'd relaxed. *Properly*. And a relaxed Owen was doubly potent.

It sent warning bells clanging through Callie's mind. All she wanted to focus on was finding a new direction in life—starting with the TV job. And then she'd make a decision about her inheritance. And she planned to do all of that footloose and fancy-free, thank you very much. She wasn't letting any man into her life until she was damn certain everything she'd worked so hard for couldn't be pulled out from under her. She wasn't putting her livelihood at the mercy of some guy's whims. She'd learned that lesson the hard way.

And she had an extra reason to worry now too. If word got out that she'd inherited so much money, how could she be certain that any man would want her for herself? How could she be certain he wasn't interested in her money instead?

Even Owen. After all, how much did she really know about him?

She glanced across at him in his soft worn jeans that looked as comfortable as air and his loose long-sleeved tee. A girl could admire a good-looking guy without it meaning anything, though, right?

'Are you sure there's nothing I can do?' she asked.

'Just keep sitting there, looking suitably impressed with my kitchen skills. It's doing wonders for my ego.'

He said it with the same teasing half-grin he used on

Lissy and it made her feel as if she belonged, that she wasn't an unwelcome intruder.

Dangerous. The word whispered through her. Still, the man prepared a salad with an elegance that was *very* easy on the eye…

'You know your way around a kitchen better than I do.'

'I like to cook. It gives me time to think. Figuring out how to make an app work can take a lot of thinking time.'

Margaret ambled over from the sofa, where she'd been flicking through a newspaper, to perch on a stool beside Callie. Lissy and Barney were out in the courtyard. Callie could hear Lissy talking on her phone.

'It's something you do very well,' Margaret said. 'Your apps are inspired.'

'Obviously the company he works for thinks so,' said Callie. 'I saw his office. It's amazing.'

Margaret sent her son a swift glance, but he was busy slicing onions. 'He's too modest,' she said drily.

Callie did her best not to get mesmerised by the sight of those large hands, with their short, slightly squared nails, effortlessly slicing and chopping.

'Coming up with ways to make a lecture or a tutorial engaging and fun can be a bit like that,' she said. 'But doing my thinking time in the kitchen would be a disaster. The food would either be half raw or burned to a crisp.'

His grin hooked up one side of his mouth and her heart started pitter-pattering away as if it had donned tap shoes and was learning a brand-new dance routine. He scattered sliced red pepper over the lettuce and red onion already in the salad bowl before adding cherry tomatoes and sliced cucumber. She blinked when he pulled extra virgin olive oil and a bottle of gourmet vinegar from the pantry.

He made his own dressing?

The fork he whisked with faltered for a moment as he

sent her a sidelong glance, and she suddenly realised she was staring. She had to get over this awareness. It was crazy!

She swung to Margaret. 'What's the thing you remember most about Frances?'

A sigh Callie didn't understand eased out of the older woman. 'I have a lot of memories. But honestly…? It's her sadness I find myself remembering most.'

Owen stopped whisking and stared at his mother as if her words had speared straight through his heart.

She sent Callie a small smile. 'Frances helped me escape an unpleasant situation and I'll be forever grateful to her. I loved her. I just wish I could've done…more.'

She reached out to touch Margaret's arm. 'I'm glad she was able to help you. But from what Owen has told me, you all helped her tremendously too.'

Margaret nodded. 'Owen especially.'

Really? She filed that under her *Things to Pursue Later* list.

'I also remember her political rants,' Margaret added with a laugh. 'She could be scathing when she disagreed with whoever happened to be in power at the time. Hilariously so. She'd have us all in stitches, but nodding in agreement.'

'That sounds like fun.' And it did.

Margaret nibbled a piece of cucumber Owen had pushed her way, as if he was inherently attuned to what she'd like. He glanced at Callie and raised an eyebrow. She pointed to the red pepper, so he cut a nice long slice, speared it on the end of the knife and held it out to her. It made her feel ridiculously cared for.

Margaret gestured towards her son. 'Owen did most of the cooking in our household from the age of twelve onwards.'

Her eyebrows flew upwards. 'Really?'

'Mom worked long hours. Cleaning houses all day is hard work. It seemed the least I could do.'

'He traded me chores—told me he'd cook if I did the dishes.'

'Doing the dishes is my least favourite chore ever. Besides…' he grinned at his mother '…back then Mom had three standard meals that she cooked on rotation.'

Margaret winked at Callie. 'And he wasn't a fan of any of them.'

'And she'd cook them up in these huge batches, so we'd be eating the same thing for days on end. I like variety.'

His shoulders lifted in a careless shrug and Callie tried to not let her mind dwell on other things that involved variety—things she really shouldn't be thinking about.

'So you taught yourself to cook?' she said in a rush, hoping it would hide where her thoughts had gone.

He and Margaret shared a swift glance, a beat of silence passing between them, and Callie found herself nodding.

'Frances taught you how to cook.'

They both turned, as if concerned the revelation might upset her.

'It's okay,' she said, touched that they didn't want to hurt her feelings. 'You can't miss something you never knew you had.'

'Not true.' Owen rinsed the fork before turning back and searching her face.

She thought of the little boy who'd probably been terrified of his father. He'd have missed his parents not having a harmonious marriage. He'd have missed not having a father who couldn't control his temper.

'You can,' she agreed slowly.

She flashed to an image of her ten-year-old self, sitting in her classroom on Grandparents' Day. It was a memory that stuck with her to this very day.

'Do you guys do Grandparents' Day at school? It's where

grandparents spend half a day at school in the classroom with their grandkids. I wasn't the only kid in my class who didn't have grandparents, but the split would've been about eighty-twenty. And on that day I *really* wanted grandparents. And aunts and uncles and cousins and siblings and everything in between.'

She smiled, but a thread of sadness for her younger self remained. She'd yearned for big family picnics and huge Christmas celebrations and spending holidays with people who belonged to her.

'At the end of the day I raced home and told my mother that if she married again and gave me a stepfather, I would adopt his mum and dad as my grandparents.'

Owen leant his hip against the bench. 'What did she say?'

'She asked me what would happen if she fell in love with a man who didn't have parents any more, just like—' She pulled up short, suddenly conscious of how callous that would sound to Owen and Margaret—people who had loved Frances.

'Just like her,' Owen finished. He shook his head. 'It's okay, Callie.'

Actually, it wasn't. But she pasted on a smile anyway. 'I told her she was only allowed to fall in love with a man who had a mum and a dad and six brothers and sisters, all with little kids, so I could have first cousins and second cousins and third cousins twice removed.'

Margaret's eyes twinkled. 'Did she manage to keep a straight face?'

'Not for a moment!' Callie laughed. 'Though I didn't understand at the time why she thought my plan so funny.'

'When I met Jack—Lissy's father—Owen was fourteen at the time, and he took him into the courtyard out there and told him that if he ever raised either his hand or his voice to me he'd drop his cold, dead body in the river.'

Callie clapped both hands over her mouth. 'You didn't!'

His grin had her heart setting off on another tap-dancing routine. 'I obviously had an over-inflated sense of my own power. Jack weighed twice what I did, and he had arms like—' He made a big circle in the air the size of a pumpkin.

She swallowed. 'What did he say?' And where was Jack now?

'He said that if he ever did either of those things he'd help me find the best spot in the river to dump his cold, dead body.'

She pressed her hands to her chest. 'Perfect answer.'

Margaret took the salad to the small dining table as Owen lifted chicken breasts in a fancy salsa from the oven. He sent Callie a wink. 'You'll be pleased to know there has never been cause to find that spot on the river. Jack is at his monthly poker night tonight. He'll be sorry to have missed meeting you. He and Frances became great friends.'

It appeared then that everyone had been on the best of terms with Frances. Everyone, that was, except her mother.

'I've contacted three of Frances's oldest friends.'

Callie had been kneeling on Owen's living room rug, greeting Barney after returning from the library, but she shot to her feet again now. 'Friends?' *Old friends?*

'Childhood friends.'

It was three days since she'd had dinner with Owen and his family. She flew across to the breakfast bar. 'Do you think they'll talk to me? Maybe let me visit them?'

He glanced up from pouring coffee beans into his machine. 'I've organised for us to meet with them at the Russian Tea Rooms for high tea this Friday at two o'clock. It was the only time I could get them together at the same time, and I thought it'd be better to meet as a group. Their memories might spark off each other.' He halted. 'I hope that's okay? I wasn't trying to be high-handed—'

'Of course you weren't.' She reached out to squeeze his arm. 'I'm really grateful.'

Beneath her hand, his forearm burned warm and vibrant, and a bolt of energy transferred itself from him to her, making her breathe deeper and adding colour to all the things in his kitchen, as if her eyes were seeing them in a more vivid light. She suddenly felt more alive than she could remember feeling. *Ever*.

He'd stilled at her touch and he stared down at her hand now. 'We have a deal. And I mean to keep my side of the bargain, Callie.'

She reefed her hand back. That was what this was all about—the bargain they'd struck. He didn't want her short-changing the residents of the apartment block. Nothing more. Which was exactly as it should be. But her heart gave a sick thud all the same.

'I'm still grateful. Thank you.'

He shrugged, his attention on the coffee machine again and thankfully not on her.

'Hopefully they'll be able to provide you with a couple of leads.'

She hoped so too.

'Coffee?' he asked.

'Um…no thanks.' She'd shared one with him yesterday, and the day before too, but she couldn't let herself get too comfortable and cosy with him. Men were off her agenda for the foreseeable future. Her sole focus was to get that TV job and find a new direction for her life.

If you keep your inheritance you can take things easy, take your time, have a holiday…

She shook the thought off. She still intended to work. Sitting around in the lap of luxury might sound appealing at first, but she had to do *something* or she'd go out of her mind with boredom. She had no intention of being a good-for-nothing layabout. She pulled in a breath. Bottom line—

no guys until she was once again gainfully employed and her life felt as if it belonged to her again.

She edged towards the door. 'I might just dump my gear upstairs and then take Barney for a walk.'

She didn't ask him if he wanted to join her. They weren't friends. All she was to him was a duty to discharge.

'C'mon, Barney.'

The little dog scrambled to his feet and scurried across the room to her. The two of them had started towards Owen's front door when Owen called out, 'What do you do at the library, Callie?'

Working at the library sounded romantic—as if she might be sitting in a lofty vaulted room poring over dusty tomes, but the reality was vastly different.

'Basically I just use their computers to access genealogical databases and old newspapers…and print off whatever looks useful.'

'You could do that from here.'

'Except my laptop was taken in the robbery. And as I have access to my emails on my phone, I figured I wouldn't bother replacing it until I got home.'

'I have a spare computer you can use.'

The day she'd been in his office he'd had three computers all fired up and on the go at the same time. She'd figured they were all necessary for whatever it was he did. Besides, the thought of working beside him day after day…

She shook her head. 'I've intruded enough on your time as it is, Owen. You don't need me under your feet. The library is fine.'

He stared, and then his eyes widened and his mouth puckered as if he'd sucked on a lemon. 'I wasn't suggesting you work in my office.'

She folded her arms and raised an eyebrow. *Nice.*

'Sorry, but I'm not good with distractions—noise,

music…other people moving about. It breaks my concentration.'

She unbent a fraction and glanced at Barney.

Owen shook his head. 'Barney is as good as gold. He just lies on his bed—' they'd both bought Barney dog beds for their respective apartments '—and we enjoy each other's company.'

'You're such a good dog,' she cooed, scratching Barney's hindquarters until he groaned his pleasure.

Owen frowned. 'He doesn't chew anything he shouldn't. He doesn't bark when he hears any of the other residents coming or going…'

'And on walks he's always polite to other dogs. He loves choosing random people to make friends with. He's sociable and well adjusted.' She blew out a breath, nodding. 'I know… *Someone* has to be missing him.'

'No word yet?'

'None.' She checked the posters they'd put up in various shop windows and on trees in the park every time she and Barney went for a walk. Just to make sure they were still there and didn't need replacing.

'Okay—back to the subject of the computer. I was going to suggest we set up a spare computer and printer in your apartment. You're welcome to use it for as long as you're in New York.'

She swiped her hands down the sides of her jeans. 'Are you sure you can spare one?'

'You *have* seen my office, right?'

His hands went to his hips and it made him look tall and broad and delectable. Her tongue stuck to the roof of her mouth. She did her best to unglue it. 'If you can spare it, then a computer would be very welcome.'

'Done. Let's do it.'

He strode into his office and she followed in his wake, slightly bemused.

'Can you manage the printer?' He opened a door to a storage cupboard and effortlessly lifted out a printer. 'If not I can make a second trip.'

'Give it here. Of course I can manage. I'll head on up and open the door,' she added as he started to haul out a computer. And cables.

'I'll be right behind you.'

The printer wasn't heavy, but by the time she'd climbed the stairs she was short of breath.

'I need to get fitter, Barney.'

But she knew there was nothing wrong with her fitness levels. It was just that the guy downstairs had a habit of stealing all the oxygen from her lungs, and it always took too long for her to get it back.

Callie's face when they entered the Russian Tea Room was priceless. The red leather banquettes, dark green walls and twenty-four-carat gold ceiling made a striking statement— and that was before you took into account the priceless artworks on the walls.

'It's amazing,' she breathed.

Owen had wanted the three older women to feel spoiled. He's hoped it would make them more amenable to answering Callie's questions.

She swung to him. 'I will, of course, be paying for this.'

'Already taken care of,' he said, and pointed across the room to one of the red leather banquettes against the far wall to distract her. 'Josephine, Betty and Eliza are already here.'

He refused to question too closely why he'd wanted to cover the cost of today's expedition. Heaven only knew Callie now had more than enough money to cover the expense for a hundred such afternoon teas, but...

On Saturday night he'd seen something hungry in her—

something that had made him want to draw her into the warmth and ease of his family circle.

For the greater part of his childhood it had been only him, his mother and Frances. They had constituted the people he could rely on. On Saturday night he'd realised that for *all of Callie's life* it had just been her and her mother. He understood loneliness, and he'd recognised it in her.

It had made him…

He rolled his shoulders, suppressing a frown. It had made him want to pay for today's afternoon tea, that was all.

Thrusting his disturbing thoughts to one side, he set about the task of introducing Callie to Frances's contemporaries and smoothing the waters to encourage conversation. 'Callie never even knew she had a grandmother—Donna never told her—so she's hoping to get to know Frances through the memories of the people who knew her.'

Over cucumber, caviar and salmon sandwiches, and glasses of French champagne, the older women reminisced about the days when they'd all been girls together—from schoolgirls to debutantes and then society wives. Callie had told him she wanted to discover the identity of her father—that it was the main reason she wanted to meet her grandmother's friends—but that consideration seemed to go by the wayside as she hung on to their every word as if each one was pure gold…as if she couldn't get enough of their stories.

'It all changed, though, when Frances married Richard,' said Eliza.

'In what way?'

Callie nibbled a miniature lemon tart as if only mildly interested in that statement…as if it hadn't sent a quiver through her entire body. Owen suspected nobody had noticed but him.

'Did you not like Richard?' she asked.

All three women hesitated. 'It's not that,' Eliza said eventually. 'He was...very good-looking.'

Callie nodded. 'I've seen pictures. He was movie-star-handsome.'

'And charming to go with it,' Betty added. 'Maybe Frannie had been on her own too long—it took her a long time to get over Tom's death—but she completely lost her head over Richard. In her eyes, he could do no wrong.'

Callie laughed lightly, but there was no real humour in it. 'That's a rookie mistake right there, isn't it? No one's perfect.' She glanced up from pushing a crumb around her plate. 'I take it you ladies didn't trust him?'

Again there was the slightest hesitation. 'It might just be the benefit of hindsight because we now know what came after...' said Josephine.

'Frances was too giddy. It made us uneasy,' said Betty.

'And Richard's charm was too practised, too perfect,' said Eliza.

'And yet they threw the most wonderful parties, and Frannie was so sublimely happy...'

'So we kept our reservations to ourselves...'

'Not that it would've done any good to have done otherwise. Frannie wouldn't have a bad word said against him.'

All three nodded at that. Fresh tea and another tray of perfect pastries and *petit fours* that looked like works of art were delivered, momentarily halting the flow of conversation.

'What about my mother?' Callie asked when the waiter had moved away. 'Did she like Richard?'

'Heaven's no! Donna was the only one to openly criticise him. According to Frannie, she called him a liar and a cheat who was only after Frances's money.' Betty bit her lip. 'She told her mother she was making a fool of herself.'

Owen winced. So did Callie.

'It was awful. There was the most enormous row and

Frannie and Donna never spoke again. After that none of us had the courage to speak out against Richard.'

Callie rested her elbows on the table. 'So *that's* what their rift was about. It—' She hastily removed her elbows, as if suddenly remembering her manners. 'It just doesn't seem enough to cause total estrangement, though.'

'I've often thought the same thing,' said Josephine, the quietest of the three older women. 'Your mother was a lovely, bright girl—quick to laugh, but not quick to anger.'

'Frances had a hot temper, though?' asked Callie.

'All I know,' Josephine said, 'is that Donna wasn't at the wedding and Frances never uttered her name again.'

'Donna was a daddy's girl, though. Maybe she couldn't stand the notion of anyone supplanting him in Frannie's affections.'

'That hardly seems likely, Betty. Donna was an adult by then. She never struck me as the kind of girl who would demand something so unreasonable of her mother. No, I just think she saw through Richard and refused to stay quiet about it.'

'Heaven knows, none of us dared ask Frannie for details.'

Owen stared at the older women. He'd known none of this. *None.* It was as if it had happened to someone else, rather than the Frances he'd known.

A tiny smile touched Callie's lips. 'Was Frances such a tyrant, then?'

'Not at all, but she felt things deeply—too deeply, I often thought,' Josephine said. 'It was clear that whatever had passed between her and Donna had hurt her badly. It changed her—not necessarily for the better. It felt wrong to probe—unkind, even. All we could do was offer our silent support and let her know we were there for her. But I never expected their rift to last a lifetime.'

They were all silent for a moment.

'Frannie paid a heavy price for her brief happiness with

Richard…' Eliza sighed. 'They'd only been married for two years when his affairs with other women started. It was a torrid time. The fights!'

'And then what we'd all feared came to light—Richard *had* only married Frannie for her money. And it cost her a pretty penny to extricate herself from the marriage.'

'After that she changed. Became withdrawn. She moved out of her lovely Upper East Side apartment and buried herself in that apartment in Greenwich Village. Don't get me wrong,' Josephine said quickly. 'It's a lovely apartment…'

Betty nodded. 'But nothing like the one she'd been living in.'

'Fabulous location, though…' Eliza sighed.

'Not that she ever took advantage of it. She never left it.'

Here was the woman Owen had known.

'She stopped seeing everyone—all her old friends.'

'She tried to stop seeing us too, only we wouldn't let her. We were very persistent.'

'She eventually stopped being so bloody-minded and let us visit. And she interested herself in the residents of the apartment block. That helped too. But she never regained her zest for life, never recovered her spirits.'

'She once told me she'd broken her own heart—that she'd been wilful and blind and deserved her loneliness and regrets.'

A tiny breath left Callie and snagged at Owen's heart.

'Poor Frances,' she said. 'I'm so glad she had the three of you.'

Owen watched as she rallied, and he sensed the effort it cost her.

'Here's something you might not know. She wrote to my mother—many, many times over the years. My mother returned the letters unopened, but I think it was clear Frances did attempt to reconcile with her.'

Josephine smiled. 'I'm glad. I'm sorry Donna remained

so unforgiving, but I'm very glad Frances tried. Thank you for telling us, Callie.'

Conversation turned to happier times, and although Owen waited for Callie to probe more deeply about her mother, she merely sat amid the splendour of the Russian Tea Room as if in a state of suspended animation.

'Callie is looking for clues as to who her father might be. Would you ladies have any idea where she might start looking?' he said eventually.

Callie started, and then sent him a smile. Beneath the table she briefly clasped his hand in silent thanks. It made his heart double in size.

Eliza's eyes went round. 'You mean Donna was pregnant before she left the States?'

'I was born four months after she arrived in Australia,' said Callie.

'Well, I can't say I recall her dating anyone regularly.' Josephine tapped a finger to her lips. 'Though she must've met a lot of boys at college.'

The three women conferred, but all came up blank.

'Did Donna have any close girlfriends that you can recall?' she asked.

Josephine's face cleared. 'The Ryder girl! She's Hitchcock now. They were thick as thieves. I can text you her details—or, better yet, you could come visit me, Callie. I have albums full of photographs I'm sure you'd be interested in seeing.'

The party broke up with Callie promising to visit each of them.

'Are you okay?' he asked as they made their way outside.

She halted to stare at a display in a shop window, her reflection pensive and troubled, and it was all he could do not to reach out and pull her in close for a hug.

'Frances feels real to me now in a way she didn't before. Her story is so *sad*. I want to cry for her.'

No way was he taking her back to Frances's gloomy apartment just yet. 'Only the final third,' he said. 'The first two-thirds of her life sound pretty damn good if you ask me.'

She blinked.

'And, while she might've become a recluse, her life wasn't totally devoid of pleasure. She had good things even at the end. Don't forget that.'

She reached out and touched his arm. 'I'm really glad she had you and your mother and Lissy and Jack, Owen. Thank you for taking such good care of her.'

'She took good care of us too.'

His throat thickened, but he didn't know if it was grief for Frances rising through him again or the dark troubled depths of Callie's eyes catching him in some unknown but vulnerable spot deep inside.

He forced himself to straighten and smile. 'So, tell me... How much of New York have you seen since you arrived?'

'Um...not a lot. I had an amble along Fifth Avenue, because the New York Public Library is, like, right there. And I went to Times Square because... I mean it's Times Square, right? But I'm not here to sightsee.'

He feigned outrage. 'You're in one of the most vibrant cities in the world! I know you're preparing for that TV job, but you shouldn't squander the chance to experience New York while you're here. What about the Statue of Liberty, the Brooklyn Bridge, the Empire State...the Guggenheim, the High Line? There's so much to see and experience. You should make time for some of that.'

'I suppose you're right. It's just...'

'You've had other things on your mind.' He glanced at her feet. She wore a pair of comfortable-looking boots. 'Are you busy for the rest of the afternoon?'

'What did you have in mind?'

'If those boots are as comfortable as they look, how about a walk through Central Park?'

CHAPTER SIX

'THE PARK IS *HUGE*!'

Callie stared at Bethesda Fountain before moving down the grand sandstone staircase to the terrace below. She felt as if they'd left the city far behind, and some of her earlier sombreness fell away.

'It's *so* beautiful. I'm surrounded by shades of *When Harry Met Sally* and *Home Alone 2* and *Begin Again...*'

'You didn't realise the park was this big?' asked Owen.

She trailed her fingers in the water of the fountain as they strolled around it. 'I knew from looking at a map of Manhattan that it was going to be big. But actually seeing it...' She turned on the spot. 'I feel as if we could be in the country somewhere.'

They strolled for a while, ambling along beautiful paths, and Callie lapped it up, letting it soothe the burn in her chest that had sparked into life during afternoon tea as Eliza, Betty and Josephine had drawn a picture of Frances's life for her. It had been a privileged life. And to think that her mother had grown up in that same privileged world...

It seemed wrong that Callie had known nothing about it. Not that she envied it. While it fascinated her, in many ways her own childhood had been idyllic. But it was part of her beloved mother's history, and it should've become part of Callie's history too—if only by proxy.

The burn in her chest intensified when she recalled all the things Donna had foregone because money had been so tight—pretty clothes, regular visits to the salon, brand-new books...eating out. None of those things were necessities, by any means, but it didn't mean they hadn't been missed.

Her mother had scrimped and saved for the deposit to

buy her modest little house, but Callie recalled one month when they'd fallen behind on the mortgage payments. Donna had pawned her diamond earrings—the only nice jewellery she'd owned—and she could remember listening to her mother cry that night, when she'd thought Callie was asleep. The burn of hot tears that had trickled down her own cheeks had been like the burn that had embedded itself in her chest now.

But her mother's financial hardship would've ceased if she'd only opened one of Frances's letters. Why hadn't she? What had Frances done that had made Donna so determined to shut her out?

Yet she found it impossible to slide Frances into the role of villain. Hearing about her happy marriage to Thomas, and then her disastrous marriage to Richard, had brought Frances to life for her. She'd bled for the older woman— for her heartbreak and grief.

And that made her feel disloyal to Donna.

'Would you like to sit for a bit?'

Owen's voice intruded on her thoughts and she sent him a swift smile. 'Sure.'

They sat on a bench and he gestured in front of them. 'This is Conservatory Water. It's been in lots of movies too. Kids sail model boats here.'

A smile hooked up the right side of his mouth, as if he remembered doing that as a boy, and it made him look young and carefree. Her heart pressed hard against her lungs, making it ridiculously difficult to catch her breath. For a wild moment all she could wonder was what it would be like to press her lips to his.

She dragged her gaze away, her heart pounding. She needed to get over this crazy, stupid crush and be a sensible adult woman again. She focussed her attention on a jogger who moved past them at an easy pace and then realised she was staring at a celebrity.

She grabbed Owen's arm. 'Did you see who that was?' 'I did.'

He didn't sound the slighted bit fazed—as if he saw celebrities all the time. Mind you, this was New York, so maybe he did.

She stared after the celebrity—who'd starred in several of her favourite movies—and shook her head, forcing herself to release Owen's arm. 'You know, I'm not sure anyone needs to see him in bike shorts, though.'

His low chuckle warmed the surface of her skin and helped to ease some of the tension that had her wound so tight.

He turned to her. 'I want to thank you for being so kind to Lissy. She really enjoyed your shopping trip.'

'Kindness had nothing to do with it. It wasn't a chore. I enjoyed it too.' She frowned. 'I don't think you view Lissy as a chore either.'

'Of course I don't. Even if she isn't interested in hanging out with me any more.'

The disconsolate slope of his shoulders was mirrored in the downward droop of his mouth, and it caught at her. This was none of her business, but...

He sent her a smile that twisted her heart. 'Are all teenage girls difficult?'

She dragged in a breath. 'Would you like some advice where Lissy's concerned? I don't have a sister, but I have worked with a lot of young people.'

'Yes.' He said it without hesitation.

'You have to promise not to bite my head off.'

He straightened, his eyes suddenly sharp. 'Cross my heart.'

She pressed her hands together to counter her sudden insane desire to touch him. 'Owen, I honestly think you'd be better served acting like Lissy's fun older brother than...um...'

'A disapproving maiden aunt? That's what she called me on Saturday.'

Which was hardly surprising. She'd watched him. He hadn't tried to hide his disapproval at what Lissy had been wearing. He'd scowled in the most ferocious way whenever Lissy had mentioned the name of any male friend. Lissy had predictably responded with snark and attitude. Callie understood both points of view, but...

'I'd bet a year's salary—' she huffed out a mirthless laugh '—except, of course, I'm not currently earning a salary.'

'But you will be soon.'

His words were clear and sure, and they made her shoulders go back. Of course she would. 'Anyway, I'd bet Lissy only pulls her short skirts out of her wardrobe...and mentions the names of so many boys...just to get a rise out of you. She bought a couple of things on Saturday—items of clothing of which I'm sure you'd wholeheartedly approve. But I doubt she'll wear them if she thinks you're going to see them.'

He stared. 'Why not?'

'And, while boys were certainly mentioned during our shopping day,' she continued, 'they by no means formed the major part of our conversation. We talked about girl-friends and books and movies and so many other things.' Things she'd noticed Lissy hadn't mentioned around Owen.

'So...she's not obsessed with boys?'

'No more than any other sixteen-year-old girl. And I've got to tell you, Owen, you need to ease off a bit or you're going to smother her with disapproval.'

His mouth tightened.

'I know it comes from a good place. From a desire to protect her...'

'Of course I want to protect her! I know how ugly the

world can be. I don't want her ever to suffer the way my mother did.'

Oh, Owen. He hadn't been able to protect his mother so he was determined to protect his little sister.

She blinked hard against the burn in her eyes. 'But Lissy has Margaret and Jack, who both sound smart and savvy. They aren't neglectful, are they? They love her? You trust them, don't you?'

'Of course I do!'

'Then leave the parenting to them.'

His jaw dropped.

'Both you *and* Lissy would be better served if you were the approachable big brother she could confide in without fear of being judged or having her head snapped off.'

He ran a hand over his face. 'You make me sound like the worst of grumps.'

'I know you're not. And deep down Lissy does too. But she's a teenager. At her age everything takes on an added edge that can feel pointed and overwhelming. She thinks you don't trust her.'

His gaze speared to hers and she shrugged.

'Imagine how that makes her feel.'

Very slowly he nodded.

She hesitated, but those grey eyes were on her in a heartbeat, sharpening at whatever they saw in her face.

'There's more?' he asked.

Help! She was about to embark into truly personal territory. 'She mentioned someone called Fiona…'

His head reared back and it took all her courage to continue.

'I got the impression she's an old girlfriend of yours.'

He gave the briefest of nods.

'I also got the impression that something happened between the two of them.'

Everything about him went on high alert. 'Do you know what?'

She shook her head. 'But if you decide to raise the topic—*when* you decide to raise the topic,' she amended, because she could see that he fully intended to do so, 'tread carefully. Instinct tells me she really hurt Lissy's feelings.'

Her stomach churned at his sudden pallor and the self-recrimination reflected in his eyes.

'I expect Fiona didn't mean to cause any harm, but—'

'Then you'd expect wrong.'

The ice in his voice had a chill chasing down her spine.

'Fiona and I were engaged.'

What? To be *married*?

'But she wasn't the woman I thought she was. It never occurred to me she'd take her anger out on Lissy.' His lips twisted. 'Evidently I was too caught up in my own pity party.'

'I'm sorry, Owen. I—'

'You've nothing to apologise for. I appreciate all you've said.' He nodded. 'And I will tread carefully. But I *am* going to fix this.'

He clasped her hands briefly, and she could see something inside him had lightened.

'Thank you.'

She found a smile of her own. 'Well…thank *you* for organising today's meeting. It was great to meet Frances's friends.'

'I was happy to help.' He sobered again, his brow creasing. 'But the woman Josephine, Betty and Eliza described today…the Frances from those earlier years…is a stranger to me. She sounded so vibrant and full of life…'

It hadn't occurred to Callie how her quest might affect him. She didn't want to mar his memory of his godmother. He'd *loved* Frances. She ached to reach out and squeeze his arm in silent sympathy and let him know he wasn't alone. But she hesitated too long and the moment passed.

His frown deepened. 'What happened between her and Richard seemed to break her.'

'I wonder why, though. I know love can be a tricky thing, but...'

His snort told her he considered that an understatement.

'But Frances sounded like a strong woman,' she said.

'Your point being?'

She pressed her hands together, gazing at the column of his throat rather than meeting the misty grey of his eyes.

'Very few of us manage to get through life without making a fool of ourselves romantically at least once, right?'

There was an intriguing sprinkle of hair at the vee of Owen's shirt and— *Stop it!* She deliberately made herself think of Dominic and familiar anger flared in her chest.

'I sure as hell have. And, after what you just said about Fiona, I guess you have too.'

'Yep.'

She swallowed at the way his lips thinned. There was a story there, but she refused to ask about it.

'But most of us don't turn into recluses because of it. Frances made a mistake about Richard—' just as Callie had with Dominic '—but so what?'

Owen blinked.

'I'm not saying that to be callous. I don't doubt he hurt her really badly. But I still don't get it.'

'Josephine said she felt things too deeply. And she *did* marry her mistake. We didn't marry ours, and that has to make a difference.' He stilled. 'At least *I* didn't.'

She shook her head, barely suppressing a shudder. 'Me either.'

'She trusted Richard and he abused that trust. What he did was despicable.'

'You won't get any argument from me about that. It's clear he broke her heart and disillusioned her. But did he break her spirit too? We've just agreed she was a strong woman, and it's clear that she had access to a lot of resources, so why turn herself into a modern-day Miss Havisham?'

'What are you thinking?'

'That thing Betty said about Frances breaking her own heart... What if it wasn't Richard she was referring to?' The thought formed as she spoke. 'What if it was whatever happened between her and my mother?'

He was silent for several long moments. 'If you're right,' he finally said, 'you could be opening a huge can of worms.'

Her heart sank. Maybe she should let sleeping dogs lie.

'You must want this job badly...'

The job! She straightened. Of course she wanted the job. Of course she was going to prise the lids off all cans that needed jemmying.

'So what now?' he asked.

She pulled in a breath to bolster her resolve. 'Josephine is going to text me the details of my mother's friend. As soon as she does I'll arrange a meeting. Hopefully she'll know the truth and will be willing to share it. If not, then maybe she suspects something or can toss me a bone. If she doesn't...' She trailed off.

He leaned his elbows on his knees and stared at the boat pond. Three children were sailing remote-controlled boats and Callie couldn't help thinking it looked like fun.

'You also have the letters, so there's a chance you could find a clue there. Or maybe even the truth.'

Except so far she hadn't had the courage to open them. Dread flooded her every time she picked one up. Callie was an adult now. Her mother didn't get to make decisions for her any more. But there had to be a good reason she'd never told Callie about Frances—and a good reason why she'd never been reconciled with her mother.

Opening them felt disloyal. And a part of her was scared—scared that she'd come to like Frances. And she didn't want to like someone who'd done something awful to her mother. She wanted to find out what had happened between the two women first. She'd relegated reading those letters to being her last course of action.

'You said you wanted to video yourself talking to the camera and explaining how you've traced your family tree from the few seeds you've been thrown?' Owen said.

Glad for the distraction, she nodded.

'Then how's this for a plan? I could rearrange my work schedule, and one day next week we could head up to Ellerslie. The house is currently vacant, but there's a care-taker couple who've worked there for years. We could have a rummage around and maybe film on location there. We'll probably have to stay overnight at a nearby inn, but that shouldn't be a problem.'

Her whole body became electrified at the thought—*visit the family estate?*

'Have you ever been there?' she asked. 'It looks stunning. The photographs are amazing...'

'I had no idea Frances even owned an estate until after her death.'

'It'd be wonderful to do some filming there—it would add a real wow factor. Are you sure we're allowed?'

'I'm the executor of Frances's will. If your mother refuses her inheritance I'm going to have to oversee the sale of the property. At some point I'm going to have to inspect it to see if any work needs to be done.'

'What about your boss? Won't he mind? Can you just take off like that?'

He glanced up into the blue of the sky and she figured he was mentally tallying up his work schedule.

'I can swing it,' he said finally.

To have that kind of leeway and freedom at work had to mean that he was seriously good at his job—that his employer was willing to give him the world in order to keep him. That was what *she* wanted—to be so good at something, so competent, that her job would never be in jeopardy again.

'And you're sure it'd be okay for me to tag along?'

How would her mother feel about Callie visiting Ellerslie?

Owen leaned forward to clasp her hands, as if sensing the tug of war going on inside her. 'As your mother's deputy, I'd have thought you have an obligation to see the house.'

'But my mother hasn't made me her deputy,' honesty forced her to point out.

He hesitated. 'You've kept those letters that Donna returned because you think she needs to read them. In that same spirit you have to see the estate so you can give her… I don't know…a report on it. At least take some photos to send her.'

That made sense. 'You want her to accept her inheritance, don't you?'

He hesitated, and then nodded. Then, 'Can I ask you something? Why consider rejecting your inheritance when Frances has put no conditions on it? I don't understand your reasoning. Why not just accept it and treasure it as the gift it is?'

Callie knew he saw it as his honour-bound duty to ensure Frances's wishes were fulfilled. And in the service of that he'd put pressure on Callie to accept her inheritance. His loyalty belonged to Frances, not her.

She pulled in a breath. 'If something really bad happened between Frances and my mother—and I think it's pretty clear something did—if Frances treated my mother cruelly… Then to accept my inheritance would be…' she searched her mind for the right words '…tacit approval for whatever it was she did. Accepting her money would be like taking a bribe to turn a blind eye to the past.'

If Frances had treated Donna reprehensibly, then she'd show solidarity with her mother. She'd turn her back completely on Frances and her world of wealth and privilege.

'I think both you and your mother have misjudged Frances.'

And after hearing about Frances today... 'A part of me hopes you're right,' she said.

Frances's story had struck a chord with her—maybe because of her own ill-fated love affair—and she felt as if she had a lot in common with the other woman. Just as Frances had thought with Richard, Callie had believed she'd have everything she'd ever wanted—family, children, financial stability, love—with Dominic. Both she and Frances had been cruelly disillusioned.

'It may all turn out to be nothing more than a big misunderstanding,' said Callie. And if that were the case then she might be able to make things right.

'Callie, you have a right to visit the estate. It's your family history too.'

She lifted her chin. It was.

For the time being she'd concentrate on the simplest of her current concerns—the TV job. She had every intention of applying for it, regardless of whatever else happened, and video footage of the estate would add serious drama to her little documentary.

She rubbed her hands together. 'That job is *so* mine. My documentary is going to knock the interview panel's socks off.'

He grinned back. 'Look, I know you're all over this video of yours, but don't forget I'm a tech nerd, with some serious hardware back at my apartment.'

Her heart gave a giant kick. 'You'd help me turn my little home video into something seriously slick?'

He raised his hands skyward. 'I thought you'd never ask.'

'Oh, Owen, thank you!'

Their gazes caught and held in a moment that, for Callie at least, was pure exhilaration. She found herself falling into the warm smoky depths of Owen's eyes.

Very slowly those delectable smiling lips of his sobered at whatever he saw reflected in her face. His gaze lowered to her lips and a tic started up inside her when the smoke darkened to midnight and she recognised his raw hunger.

He wanted her! Owen wanted her every bit as much as she wanted him.

The knowledge lifted her up as if on the crest of a wave—and exhilaration, delight, and the most delicious anticipation thrilled through her, because she knew he was about to kiss her. And she had every intention of meeting that kiss with an enthusiasm that left him in no doubt as to how much she wanted him.

She swayed towards him as his head lowered towards hers. One of her hands landed on his shoulder, the other rested against his chest. His body was absurdly firm, and so throbbing with life that her fingers automatically curled and then flattened in an effort to feel more of him.

And then his lips were on hers and their warmth took her off guard—warmth as in heat, but warmth as in feeling too. He kissed her as if he couldn't think of anything else he'd rather be doing, and she couldn't resist the allure of being so wholly and wholeheartedly relished.

She kissed him back with the same undiluted appreciation and a groan rasped from the back of his throat. That was the moment she lost all sense of herself. Her hands tunnelled through his hair to pull him closer and his hands went around her back, one coming up to cradle her head and hold her still so he could kiss her with a sweeping thoroughness that left her lost to everything except the moment and the rightness of being with him.

She had no idea how long they kissed, but they eventually broke apart to drag air into sawing lungs.

She hung there, suspended between heartbeats…

A shrill and sudden noise intruded on the spring quiet, making her start and Owen freeze. It took her a moment to realise it was her phone, and by the time she'd grabbed it from her handbag Owen had marched across to the pond, his back ramrod-straight.

She stood and pressed the phone to her ear. 'Hello?'

She listened as the voice of the man at the other end explained who he was. She made all the appropriate responses, hoping she didn't sound as shell-shocked and topsy-turvy as she felt, an ocean of need still stampeding through her.

Owen turned to her when she rang off. She didn't know what to make of that kiss, or Owen's reaction now. Was he regretting the interruption? Or was he grateful for it? If it was the latter, she didn't want to be anywhere near him. Not until she had her game face well and truly back into place.

'Callie, that kiss...'

He bent at the waist and braced his hands against his knees. Her heart plummeted, but she refused to let her chin drop.

'Was amazing,' she finished for him.

His gaze speared back to hers and she recognised the wariness in his eyes...and the regret. Acid coated her tongue. But a moment later she shook herself. Of *course* he regretted it. She regretted it too. What on earth had she been thinking? She *hadn't* been thinking!

She swallowed and forced herself to continue. 'But I'm not in the market for anything like that at the moment. I don't want a short-term fling, and anything long-term is just—' she dragged a hand through her hair '—unthinkable. I—'

He straightened. 'You don't need to explain, Callie.'

She didn't?

'I feel the same. Fiona and I broke up eight months ago, but it still feels too soon to start something new.'

Her heart gave a strange little twist. 'That makes perfect sense. You were going to marry her. That takes some...'

Gah, why hadn't she simply stopped at *That makes perfect sense*? 'Some time to readjust,' she finished lamely.

He stared at her. 'So…we're good?'

'Absolutely.' She waved at the bench. 'That was just a blip. One of those "less said, soonest mended" things.'

'Agreed.' His relief was palpable. 'Then we'll just consider it forgotten.'

She had a feeling it wasn't going to be that easy. At least not for her.

Pushing the thought aside, she held up her phone. 'That was Mr Singh. A gentleman who claims he's Barney's owner.'

'Barney's owner?'

'He's in hospital. I said we'd go and visit him.'

He blinked.

'I mean,' she amended hastily, '*I'll* go and visit him, you don't have to come.'

'Of course I'm coming. I've been sharing custody, remember?'

'We should really drop by the apartment to make sure Barney's okay. Maybe take him out for a bit.'

They'd left him in Owen's apartment.

'You walked him this morning. He'll be fine for another couple of hours.'

'Do you think we could smuggle him into the hospital with us? I bet Mr Singh would love to see him and—'

'No.'

But his lips twitched as he said it, and things started to feel more comfortable between them again. Her pulse was slowly returning to normal.

She told him the name of the hospital and he gestured towards the path they should take.

CHAPTER SEVEN

CALLIE WORE THE softest woollen sweater in butter-yellow and a striped scarf in mint-green and orange. She looked like a summer day in spring, but the moment she slid into the car beside Owen he knew something was wrong.

Yeah, idiot, you kissed her!

It was five days since their afternoon tea and their walk in the park. And that kiss. Of course she was going to be stand-offish. She'd made it clear she didn't want a repeat performance.

He gripped the steering wheel so hard his knuckles turned white. What on earth had possessed him to kiss her? He'd asked himself that same question over and over, but still couldn't come up with a satisfactory answer. Nor could he dredge up a satisfactory amount of regret. The kiss itself had been sensational. Not that it could happen again.

Irritatingly, he found he could dredge up more than enough regret about that.

He ground his back molars together. *That* was why he had to play it cool now. After exchanging a brusque greeting with her, he focussed his attention on the traffic and getting out of the city. The family estate of Ellerslie was in Cooperstown, nearly four hours away, and they were aiming to arrive by lunchtime.

Callie made no effort at small talk, and she only turned every now and again to check on Barney, who dozed in his crate on the back seat.

He glanced across when they were finally free of the city, his index fingers tapping on the steering wheel. Was it just that kiss or was something else on her mind?

'I didn't think to ask, but do you get car sick?'

'No.' She hunkered down further in her seat, arms folded. 'Though I still don't know what was wrong with taking the train. I checked, and it would've been fine for us to take Barney.'

'We'll have more freedom with the car.' He fought a frown. 'Besides, Barney will be far more comfortable in the car than he'd be on a train.'

They'd discovered that Mr Singh, Barney's owner, lived a short walk from the apartment block. The elderly man wasn't due out of hospital for another week. They'd assured him they'd be delighted to continue looking after Barney till then.

Owen tried coaxing her out of her odd mood. 'How many times have you been to see Mr Singh this week?'

'Every day,' she answered, as if it were the most stupid question ever asked. 'He needs someone to coax him to go for his twice-daily walks. Anyway, he's good company.'

And Owen wasn't?

He tried to quash that thought. It was pathetic, being jealous of a man who was old enough to be Callie's grandfather. Besides, he wasn't jealous. Mr Singh was minus one kidney. He'd just been through a major operation. With Callie to bear him company, though, Owen didn't doubt Mr Singh would now make great strides forward in his recovery.

Callie might not realise it, but she was a lot like her grandmother. She saw a need and rushed to meet it—whether it involved stray dogs, high school seniors wrestling with math problems, or lonely old men.

'I've dropped in on Mr Singh's neighbour a couple of times too—the one who was supposed to be looking after Barney. She felt so bad about him getting away from her... She'd been scouring the streets for him.'

'Didn't she see the posters?'

'She's seventy-seven. If she wasn't wearing her glasses...

I know what you're doing, you know—you're trying to distract me.'

The collar of his polo shirt—a staid and boring navy—tightened. 'From what?'

'Of you going to the trouble and expense of hiring a car!'

Was that what had been bothering her? 'No trouble. No expense. Callie, this is a company car.'

As he owned the company, he technically owned the car. Not that Callie knew that. He'd made damn sure she had no idea. But the lie was starting to rankle.

He opened his mouth. He closed it again. His financial situation had no bearing on their relationship. Besides, what they had wasn't a relationship. It was an…association. He and Callie had made a deal. As soon as she got this job he'd never see her again. He'd buy the apartment block. And everyone would be happy.

Unbidden, the memory of their kiss rose through him. If he hadn't been driving he'd have closed his eyes to try to shut it out. If she hadn't been sitting beside him, he'd have sworn out loud.

It had just been a kiss—nothing more—a crazy, impulsive moment that had been brief and perfect. He told himself part of its perfection was due to its very transience.

Yet that hadn't stopped the kiss from being on a slow-motion replay in his mind for the last five days. Five days in which he'd barely seen her. Oh, she'd dropped Barney off whenever she went out. And she'd been going out a lot. But she hadn't volunteered to tell him where she was going and he'd refused to ask.

He gripped the steering wheel. He had to stop thinking about that kiss and he needed to get their…*association* back on an even keel.

Before he could come up with a neutral topic of conversation she closed her eyes. He didn't know if she was feigning sleep or not, but he let her be.

Damn! She'd been so excited about filming at the estate and now she could barely stand to look at him.

When she stirred an hour later, he had a question ready for her. 'Hey, sleepy-head, I've been meaning to ask—did you get a chance to meet with your mother's friend? The Ryder woman?'

'Hitchcock now—Melissa Hitchcock.' She stretched and straightened. 'I met with her yesterday. She seems lovely, and was really pleased to see some up-to-date photos of my mother…asked me to send her best, et cetera. But as for shedding any light on my paternity…'

'No luck?' That would explain her low spirits.

'She thought my best bet would be to talk to Richard.'

'Donna hated Richard. Why did Melissa think he could help?'

She pushed her hands through her hair. 'She said he always seemed to know a lot about other people's business.'

Charming.

She was quiet again for a long time. Several times Owen opened his mouth to ask if anything was wrong, but shut it again. If they were friends, he'd ask. If they hadn't kissed, he'd ask. But they weren't, and they had, so he didn't.

'Did you organise those painters?' she finally blurted out. 'Three men showed up before we left this morning, saying they'd been hired to paint the interior of my apartment.'

'Finally!' He feigned exasperation. 'The apartment should've been painted weeks ago. Frances refused to have it done while she was alive—didn't want her peace disturbed. She hated having tradesmen of any kind in the place. I'm sorry, I didn't think to warn you.'

She stared out through the front windscreen, her hands gripping her opposite elbows. 'I rang Mr Dunkley. He knew nothing about it, though he told me the firm was a reputable one that he'd often used and recommended.'

Damn. He hadn't thought to clue the lawyer in.

'Then I rang the firm to find out when they'd been booked, and they told me it was a rush job and they'd only been hired on Monday.'

He grimaced. *Sprung.*

She stared at him. 'So it *was* you. You want to tell me why?'

Things inside him knotted. 'Are you mad at me?'

'I don't know yet.'

Why would she be mad at him? He'd organised it for her benefit.

'The truth is it *should've* been done before you arrived in New York…'

'But you didn't want to change things.' She turned to face him fully. 'That's understandable. You were grieving.'

'But seeing you in the apartment—getting used to seeing you there—has made me realise how damn gloomy the place is. You're spending a lot of time in it—working, living, sleeping there. You deserve something better than a…a dreary brown box.'

He'd been about to say *prison*, but checked himself. It wasn't a prison. And he refused to think of it as a prison for Frances either. It had been a haven.

'Why did you lie about it being something you'd organised ages ago?'

His collar threatened to cut off his air supply. 'I didn't want you feeling it was a nuisance or that I was going to a lot of bother—which I wasn't, by the way.' He glanced at her briefly then back at the road, and swallowed. 'I didn't want you refusing and putting up with all that depressing brown. I didn't want you getting into a funk.'

Something flashed through her eyes and her lips briefly flattened. A bad taste stretched through his mouth.

'I'm sorry. I should've been upfront with you. But it's

been an emotional time and…' His words petered out.
'You're mad.'

'I'm not mad.'

He didn't believe her.

'I'll be glad to be rid of the brown. It was nice of you
to think of it.'

All he'd done since Callie had landed in New York was
think about her. He stretched his neck, first to the left and
then to the right. As soon as she started her new job and
her new life things would return to normal.

'But…' she said.

Something in her tone had everything inside him clenching twice as hard.

'Can I ask you not to make any more decisions like that?
I know you're Frances's executor, but for the time being at
least the apartment belongs to me. I should be the one to
make any decisions about it. I mean, what if I'd organised
painters myself?'

He stiffened.

She huffed out a laugh. 'Relax! I haven't. It seemed too
much trouble to go to when the future is still so uncertain.'

He tapped his fingers against the steering wheel. '*This*
is what's been bugging you since you hopped in the car?'

'Technically it's been bugging me since the painters
knocked on my door.'

'Why didn't you have this out with me earlier instead
of sitting there stewing in silence?'

'If your actions had been mean-spirited, Owen, I'd have
raked you over the coals before I even entered the car. But
you organising the painters *wasn't* mean-spirited. You were
trying to look after me in the same way you do with Lissy.'

'But it's still irked you?'

'Because I'm a grown up! You took a decision *I* should
be making out of my hands. You've no right to do that!'

He snorted. 'You *sure* you're not mad?'

Her eyes flashed and he berated himself for poking at her.

'Sorry...'

From the corner of his eye he saw her haul in a deep breath, as if trying to compose herself.

'I'm not long out of a relationship with a man who...'

He found himself gripping the steering wheel too hard again. 'Who what?' He barely recognised his own voice.

'Who tried to rob me of my power. Who almost succeeded.'

He swung to her, appalled. 'I wasn't trying to do that.'

'I know—which is why I'm not mad. I know you're looking out for me because of the obligation you feel towards Frances.'

Except it was starting to feel like a whole lot more than that.

'I'm really sensitive to anyone taking advantage of me or overstepping boundaries at the moment. Normally I'd have let it pass. But after Dominic I swore to myself I'd stop being a doormat.'

He mulled her words over. 'So me going over your head to organise something you were more than capable of organising yourself...?'

'Pushed all my buttons.' She twisted her hands in her lap. 'It's not so easy to slap someone's wrist for overstepping boundaries when the service offered is kindly meant.'

He reached out and clasped her hands. The tension radiating from them told him it had taken courage for her to raise the topic and stick up for herself, to claim her power. But she'd still done it, and he admired her for it.

'You have my sincerest apologies—along with my promise to observe all appropriate boundaries from now on. I've no wish to make you feel less capable or less *anything*, Callie.'

'Thank you.'

The smile she sent him had heat gathering in his veins. He reefed his hand back, hastily reminding himself about appropriate boundaries.

'So...' She shuffled down in her seat, the movement easy and relaxed. 'Did you get my party invitation?'

It had been slipped under his door yesterday afternoon. 'Yes, thank you.'

'It'll be nice to have the apartment looking fresh for that.' She surveyed her fingernails. 'Are you going to come?'

'Wouldn't miss it for the world. Who else have you invited?'

'All the other tenants. I *so* hope they come.'

He made a vow to ensure each and every one of them turned up.

She rattled off three names in quick succession. 'They're the girls you met in the park, plus their parents.'

She'd met their *parents*?

'And I've invited your mother, Jack and Lissy. Mr Dunkley and his wife. As well as Josephine, Eliza and Betty. Melissa Hitchcock and her husband.' She waved a hand in the air. 'And a few other people.'

He started to laugh. 'Who else have you had a chance to meet?'

She gave an exaggerated eye-roll. 'A couple of librarians I became friendly with at the library...the coffee shop manager from that place on the corner.' She rubbed her hands together. 'I love a good party, don't you?'

Not really. Not that he said as much. 'Sure.'

She laughed. 'Liar. I remember—you're an island unto yourself.'

'I'm not! I—'

The gates to the estate had come into view, along with a big brass plaque with the word *Ellerslie* burned into it, and the sight of it had his protest dying in his throat.

Callie gave a funny little hiccup and swung towards him. 'Pull over.'

He did as she asked.

'Remember when we were talking in the park the other day about how you shouldn't let a broken heart turn you into a hermit?'

He remembered every pulse and nuance of their time in the park. And the seriousness of her expression now punched him in the gut.

'Would you react that way if some careless or conniving girl broke your heart?'

It struck him then that that was exactly what he had done when he'd discovered Fiona's duplicity. Not as completely as Frances, admittedly, but he'd definitely cut himself off and shut himself away. And forcing himself out in the service of helping Callie solve her family mystery felt good.

'It might send me to ground for a while—give me a chance to lick my wounds in private,' he said slowly. 'But not for good.'

It felt freeing to know that he meant it.

Callie smiled then—a real, straight-from-the-heart smile that pierced through him, sweet and pure.

'Good. You deserve better than that. We all do. I think we should make a pact in Frances's memory. A pact to never let disappointment in love or a broken heart let our worlds become smaller and narrower.'

His mouth went unaccountably dry. He had to swallow before he could speak. 'Callie, what are you afraid of? What do you think we're going to discover?'

The hand she'd held out for him to shake lowered. She stared at the ornate gates and chafed her arms. 'I don't know. That's what worries me.'

'We don't have to go through with this, you know… Maybe some secrets shouldn't see the light of day.'

'It feels too late to turn back.'

He knew what she meant, but...

She grimaced. 'It feels as if the lid on that can of worms you mentioned has been peeled halfway back already, and I can't pick up all the worms and put them back in.' Her nose wrinkled. 'That's a seriously disgusting analogy. I just mean I'll always have questions now.'

'Callie—'

'No, ignore me.' Shaking her head, she pulled in a breath. 'This is a bout of nerves—nothing more. I'm fine. It's just—' She swung towards him again. 'Owen, whatever we find out, I should hate for it to mar your memory of Frances.'

He reached out and squeezed her hand. 'You don't have to worry about me, Callie. My regard for Frances is steadfast, whatever happens.' He gestured. 'Are you ready?'

She pushed her shoulders back and nodded. 'I'm ready.'

CHAPTER EIGHT

THE DRIVE CURVED around a low hill and the house came into view as they rounded it, nestled neatly in the middle of the rise opposite. Even though Callie had seen photos of the house, coming face to face with it was still awe-inspiring.

Owen let loose a low whistle. 'Now, that's what I call an impressive piece of architecture.'

The house was a late-Georgian mansion, and its white stone gleamed in the spring sunshine, while the surrounding fields were lush with new growth, providing a perfect contrast. Further afield paddocks were neatly ploughed. It all looked fresh and clean and perfect.

He shook his head. 'This must cost a ridiculous amount in upkeep.'

Callie's research came to her rescue, helping to keep the panic from rising up and choking her. 'It pays for itself. Ellerslie has a successful dairy breeding programme. The estate also makes its own cheese. They've not won any national awards—yet—but they've been runners-up. I'm guessing that's all housed over there.'

She gestured to the cluster of large buildings some distance away to their left and then stared about. All of this now belonged to her mother. Had Donna spent a lot of time here as a girl? Did it hold fond memories for her? No memories? Bad memories?

The fact that she had no idea left her feeling bewildered. How could she not know about this part of her mother's life? She rubbed a hand over her chest. What on earth had made Donna turn her back on it so completely?

Owen pulled the car to a halt in the parking area to one

side of the house. He opened her door and stood there waiting patiently. Eventually he held out his hand. 'Callie?'

Forcing in a breath, she placed her hand in his. Warmth
flooded her where before she'd felt numb and frozen. Something else flooded her when she found herself almost chest
to chest with him—a thread of excitement and a sense of
possibility. She didn't know if it was for the estate or the
man, but she welcomed it regardless. It was better than
being numb with fear and crippled with misgivings.

She glanced up—meant to send him a smile of reassurance—but their eyes locked and everything else receded
into the background except the heat in his eyes and the firm
promise of his lips... It would be so easy to—

Barney barked his impatience at being confined to the
car, and she and Owen snapped away from each other. With
hands that shook, she let Barney out. The little dog leapt to
the ground and paused, ears alert, before giving a happy
yap and running in wide circles on the lawn.

She couldn't help but laugh. 'Looks like Ellerslie has
Barney's seal of approval.'

She turned back towards the house, careful not to look
at Owen, and found a woman she guessed to be Mrs Dunsmore, the housekeeper, waiting at the top of the steps. The
warmth of her smile welcomed them.

'You must be Callie. I'd know Donna's daughter anywhere! You look so much like her when she was a girl.'

'You knew my mother?'

'Oh, bless you, dear, yes—and don't fuss about the dog.
Dogs have always been welcome at Ellerslie. Yes, I remember your mother well. She spent a lot of time here with her
nan and pop. Those were happy days…back in a time when
the house was filled with people. But enough standing here
on the doorstep. Come in and make yourselves comfortable. I thought we'd have lunch before touring the house.'

She led them into an impressive entrance hall and

through several large rooms, including the most amazing drawing room filled with gleaming antiques, to a big bright kitchen at the back of the house. From the open back door Callie could see a farmhouse garden.

'I'll hunt up some photo albums for you if you like,' the housekeeper offered.

'I'd love that.'

'Also, the pair of you staying at the inn is nonsense. I've made up a pair of bedrooms for you. Now, don't argue. The young miss here—'

Callie? The young miss? She was twenty-seven!

'—will want to have a good poke about all the places her mother used to like. While you'll be wanting to check that the house and farm accounts are in order, Mr Perry.'

'Owen,' he corrected. 'And I'm sure they're in perfect order, with no need—'

'There's every need. My Pete has been fretting his poor old head about it ever since Mrs Frances died. He'd hate for anyone to think he's been overstepping the mark. There'll be plenty of time for everything if you stay. Besides, it'll be nice to have some young blood in the house again—even if it is only for one night.'

Owen lifted questioning brows at Callie and she nodded. 'We'd love to stay, Mrs Dunsmore. We're sorry to put you to so much trouble, but—'

'No trouble! No trouble at all.'

After a lunch of chicken soup and warmed rolls, she showed them their rooms. 'I gave you your mother's room, Callie. I thought you'd like that.'

Callie loved it.

Owen had the room next door.

After a quick tour, Mrs Dunsmore said, 'Now, I'll leave you to have a mosey around at your own pace. Dinner is at seven o'clock on the dot.'

'It's so grand,' Callie breathed, her head whirling with a million different thoughts.

How could her mother turn her back on all of this?

'The filming opportunities…' Owen said.

She swung around at his words. 'That entrance hall alone!'

'Did you see the portraits on the walls? All forebears of yours, no doubt.'

Her mind raced with possibilities. 'Mrs Dunsmore is bound to know who they all are. I wonder if she'd let me interview her for my video.'

After wandering about for over an hour, they gravitated to a library that looked as if it had come straight from the set of a Jane Austen period drama. There they found an old family bible with the Allbright family tree inside its venerable leather covers. And a bookcase beneath one of the windows that had been given over to estate accounts going back over a hundred years. On another shelf they found the various diaries and journals of different family members who'd lived here.

Callie pounced on one of the journals. 'Look at this! It's Hannah's diary. Hannah and Douglas were Frances's parents—my great-grandparents.' She opened it at random, ran her finger down the page. 'Oh! She's talking about the terrible time after Thomas's death.' She read several paragraphs. 'So sad…'

Owen came to stand behind her, smelling of soap and warm cotton and reassurance. It gave her the courage to flick to the last entries.

'Listen to this. *"Donna came to stay for a few days. She's met someone special. I can't imagine anyone being good enough for my darling granddaughter, of course, but her whole face lights up whenever she speaks of him. It's enough to gladden my heart. She's promised to bring him to visit soon. I can't wait to meet this man who has won her heart.'"*

'It's her final entry,' Owen murmured as Callie turned the page.

'Hannah and Douglas died in a car accident not long after this.'

'So...'

Something in Owen's tone had her glancing up. 'So?'

He rested a finger against the date of the final entry. 'Frances remarried only six months after this. Somewhere between this date and the wedding, Frances and Donna had their big falling out.'

True...

'And neither of them had Hannah or Douglas to turn to,' he said.

She stared as his meaning sank in. 'A lot happened in a short space of time... Both Hannah and Douglas were only children. With them gone, a whole generation of the family was lost.'

'And Frances and Donna lost the benefit of older and wiser heads.'

'You think Hannah and Douglas could've healed the breach?'

He gestured to the journal. 'I bet Hannah would've tried.'

So did Callie.

She traced a finger along the neat handwriting. 'She doesn't mention the name of my mother's beau.'

'Maybe Mrs Dunsmore will be able to shed more light.'

Over dinner that evening, Callie asked her. But, while Mrs Dunsmore clearly recalled Donna's last visit to Ellerslie, she hadn't been aware of any special beau.

'She was a lively girl, and lovely too—which meant she had a lot of admirers. But I don't recall anyone special.'

After dinner Callie returned to the library, to continue

reading Hannah's diary, while Owen hunkered down with Peter Dunsmore to go over the estate's accounts.

Unaccountably restless after only an hour of reading, Callie glanced out of the library's French doors to the huge summerhouse. Its multitude of windows twinkled in the moonlight, and on impulse she pushed through the doors and walked down to it.

The door opened at her touch. Fumbling for a light switch, she blinked as a sudden flood of brilliance blinded her. A series of chandeliers marched down the space, sparkling off the windows and turning the summerhouse into a fairyland. Callie pressed her hands to her chest and drank it in.

Heavenly!

Adjusting the dimmer switch to soften the lights, she walked the length of the pavilion, imagining the space filled with elegant guests and tables groaning under the weight of delectable party fare while a band played on the raised dais at the far end.

This would be the perfect place for a *Great Gatsby*-themed party. Or, better yet, for women in crinolines, their hooped skirts swirling as they waltzed with men in dark tail coats and white cravats.

The picture was so clear in her mind that she found herself pretending to hide her face behind a fan and swaying to imaginary music. 'Could you have this dance? Why, sir, I'd be delighted, I'm sure.'

She swept a curtsey to an imaginary partner, and was about to embark on a waltz when an amused voice in the doorway said, 'I've seen this movie. Julie Andrews in *The Sound of Music*, right?'

Owen. For no reason at all, her pulse picked up speed.

She swung round with a grin, not feeling the least embarrassed. 'Technically it was Liesl, the eldest daughter.

But as you got the movie right I won't hold the details against you.'

He moved the length of the pavilion towards her. There was a light in his eye that made her mouth dry even as his loose-limbed stride had her pulse thrumming.

He stopped in front of her, male appreciation lighting his face as his eyes roved over her. 'Ms Nicholls, you're looking an absolute picture this evening.' He swept a bow. 'Would you do me the honour of dancing with me?'

Oh, this was foolish and reckless. And impossible to resist!

She fluttered that imaginary fan. 'Why, Mr Perry, I thought you'd never ask.'

And then she was in his arms and he was sweeping her around the room as if he'd been born to it. She couldn't re-call the last time she'd danced a waltz, but her feet recalled the steps effortlessly. Beneath her hand the latent power of his body came alive and she couldn't help responding to it, her stomach softening and her breasts growing heavy.

'You dance beautifully, Mr Perry.' Heavens, was that breathless voice *hers*?

The expression in his eyes held her prisoner. They con-tinued to spin and twirl, perfectly attuned. 'So do you, Ms Nicholls.' Those grey eyes darkened and his feet slowed. 'You're beautiful…you know that?'

Those last words hadn't been spoken in the formal tones of a bygone era.

Callie desperately tried to think of some flippant quip—a comeback that would break the spell he was weaving around her. There were reasons she should resist it. But her mind had gone blank. Owen and his broad shoulders and his tempting mouth filled her vision and her mind.

They slowed to a halt, staring at each other, breathing hard.

'Callie…?'

She sensed how tightly he held himself, as if afraid that if he unclenched a single muscle he'd not be able to stop himself from sweeping her up in his arms and kissing her senseless. And she wanted that—despite all the reasons she shouldn't. She knew what he tasted like now…knew how he kissed. That was the problem. He was addictive! And she wanted more.

Standing on tiptoe, she met his hot, hungry gaze, her lips drawing closer and closer to his. She maintained eye contact, determined to draw back at his slightest indication, but his eyes dared her, the light flaring in them threatening to consume her. Finally, their lips touched, and a sigh left her as a quiver rippled down Owen's entire length.

Shaping her mouth to his, she threw caution to the wind and pressed closer, demanded more. His answer was swift and immediate. He hauled her close, took control of the kiss so completely her head swam, but she didn't need her head and she didn't need her balance. Owen held her securely and she gave in to the need that consumed her and trusted he would keep her safe.

Tearing the hem of his shirt from his jeans, she ran her hand over the flat planes of his stomach to the defined muscles of his chest. Hot. Firm. Shamelessly seductive.

Owen tore his mouth from hers to emit a low growl that only excited her more. She dragged her fingernails lightly down his chest, back to the waistband of his jeans. His body jerked, making her feel wanton, desirable…powerful.

That was before he dipped her over his arm, pushed her jumper up to her neck and suckled her nipple through the thin silk of her bra. She gasped, currents of pulsing need coursing to her very centre. She found herself almost sobbing with the need for release.

But then he halted and her mind seized up. Forcing heavy eyelids open, she blinked the fog from her eyes to meet his gaze.

'I want you, Callie. I want you more than—' He broke off, his breathing ragged, before righting her and drawing her jumper back down over breasts that throbbed. 'But I need to know this is what you want too.'

The words were an icy wash of cold reality.

He pushed a hand through his hair. 'I can't… We can't… If you're going to regret it tomorrow, then we need to stop now.'

She pressed suddenly cold hands to her overheated cheeks. She'd totally lost her head.

He closed his eyes, before giving a single hard nod. 'The expression on your face says it all.'

She gave a strangled laugh. 'All it can possibly say at the moment is how shocked I am at how completely I just lost control.'

She tottered over to the dais and sat before her legs gave out completely. He hesitated, then joined her.

She glanced at him and then at her hands. 'I've never been reckless when it comes to sex. If anything I've always overthought it…if you know what I mean.'

He nodded.

'But just then…' She covered her face with her hands.

'I lost control too, Callie.'

But he'd found it again. She doubted she'd have come to her senses in time to stop before things had—

Before they'd reached their natural conclusion!

She pulled her hands away. 'I'm horrified at the impression I've given you.'

He bent down so he could look directly into her face. 'You've given me no impression other than the fact that you're warm and lovely.'

'And a mess.' At his raised eyebrows, she continued. 'That ex I told you about—he's the reason my contract wasn't renewed. We worked together. We'd had a fight. A minor one, I thought. But apparently he took exception to

something I said, had a word in the head of faculty's ear…
and my job was suddenly history. I didn't even realise we
were no longer a couple until I was given my marching or-
ders. I guess he wanted to make a big impact.'

Owen's quick hiss of breath told her what he thought
of that.

'So I promised myself that until I had my career back
on track I'd not get involved with anyone.'

He stared at the ceiling for several long moments. 'I
understand, Callie. You don't owe me any explanations.'

But she wanted to give him one all the same. 'I know.
It's just… Even though I'm sorely tempted to blow rasp-
berries at my resolution and start something with you…'
She moistened her lips and did what she could to ignore
the yearning that pounded through her. 'If we were to start
something, and I were then to refuse the legacy Frances has
left me, I can't help feeling that would hurt you.'

'Callie—'

'And I don't want to hurt you.' She tried to find a smile.
'Besides, it was hard sticking up for myself about the painters, but it felt good, and I don't want to start backsliding—
relying on other people instead of myself. Regardless of
how much I want to kiss you, it feels like the wrong time
to be starting something with someone.'

'I'm hearing you. Ever since Fiona I haven't been in the
right headspace to start something new. She lied to me…
used me…and her viciousness once I found her out…' He
shook his head. 'I had a lucky escape.'

A lock of hair fell onto his brow, making him look suddenly young and vulnerable. Her heart turned over in her
chest.

'You once asked me if suspicion was my default setting.
It never used to be before Fiona.'

She couldn't stop herself from reaching out and squeezing his hand. He turned it over in his, lacing his fingers through hers.

'So now I'm going to tell you something I should've told you from the very beginning. The company I work for, the one you think is so eager to keep me... Well, I actually own it.'

She stared at him, trying to work out what he meant.

'I moved back into the apartment building because Frances needed more help than she'd ever admit. I used my break-up with Fiona as an excuse.'

'You were Frances's *carer*?'

'Of sorts. She didn't need full-time care, but it became necessary to check on her every day.'

He was a good man. Most men she knew would've delegated that task to a mother or sister. 'So your company... it's profitable?'

'Very.'

Her mouth went dry as she went over in her mind some of their previous conversations. 'Profitable enough to buy the apartment complex?'

'Several times over.'

She tried to stop her eyes from starting out of her head. 'Are you trying to tell me you're a billionaire?'

He grimaced. 'I guess...'

She gaped at him. 'I have a billionaire living in the basement?' And then she swallowed. 'Oh, Lord. I accused you of using Frances as a meal ticket and resenting the fact you didn't get anything in her will. But of course you didn't *need* anything.'

'I'm sorry. I...'

Why on earth had he let her make such a fool of herself?

She kept her tone light, even as things inside her shrivelled. 'Let me guess—you're self-made, right?' At his nod, she started to laugh. She couldn't help it. 'You know what?

I don't feel guilty any more about dragging you away from your computers or getting you into trouble with your boss.'

'You shouldn't feel guilty about anything! I—'

'Oh, *God*!' She swung to him. 'Fiona only wanted you for your money, didn't she?' The realisation struck her like a bolt from the blue, but she should've seen the connection immediately. 'Oh, Owen, I'm so sorry.' A bad taste coated her tongue. 'You thought I was like her…'

She tried to pull her hand from his, but he wouldn't let her.

'But now I know differently. I know you're not a gold-digger, Callie. And I'm sorry I didn't tell you the truth sooner. At first it didn't seem to matter, but now…' One broad shoulder lifted. 'Now it does. I know our relationship isn't going to develop into anything, but kissing you with that deception hanging over my head…' He stared down at their linked hands. 'It felt like a shabby thing to do. If our positions were reversed, I'd want to know the truth.' He met her gaze. 'I want you to know I trust you. I don't exactly know why, but it seems important that we get at least that much settled.'

Very slowly, she nodded. 'I'm glad I know the truth.' She pulled in a breath. 'After what Fiona did, I can even understand why you kept it from me.'

His lips twisted. 'There's a hardness in me now that never used to be there.'

That perfectly described how she'd felt ever since Dominic had betrayed her trust so badly.

He squeezed her hand. 'And you know what? No woman deserves to deal with that. I need to deal with it myself.'

Ditto, she thought.

She glanced about the summerhouse. 'I'd be lying if I said a part of me isn't disappointed that we're being so sensible, but…there are ghosts here. I can almost feel them. Did my mother dance with my father under these same chandeliers? Did they kiss? Did Frances and Richard dance here?' She swallowed, buttressing her resolve. 'And look what happened to them. It feels like a warning not to follow in their footsteps.'

After several beats he lifted his head, his eyes hooded and unreadable. 'Friends?'

From somewhere she found a smile, and while it didn't ease the burn in her body, it eased the burn in her soul. 'Yes, please.'

CHAPTER NINE

'THIS IS AMAZING!'

Callie beamed at him, and Owen did his best to check the elation her delight sent coursing through him. It was pointless getting all het up. It was pointless wondering what it would be like to make love with her or—

Stop it!

But it didn't matter how often he reminded himself of what she'd said at Ellerslie about not being ready for a relationship, he couldn't get the thought out of his mind. It didn't matter how often he told himself *he* wasn't interested in a relationship either, he couldn't stop from wondering *what if*?

And that spelled trouble.

He dragged in a breath. It had only been five days since they'd returned from Ellerslie. This feeling would fade soon enough. He just had to wait it out.

'You even have the theme music!' She clapped her hands. 'You've stitched all the sequences together so *seamlessly*. Owen, this must've taken you ages!'

'Nah,' he lied. 'I just pulled it together while I was between other jobs. Doing a bit here and there.'

He'd spent a ridiculous amount of time on her video. He'd enjoyed watching her animated face on the screen and the quick, expressive movements that she made with her hands as she explained how she was unravelling the mystery of her family tree.

He'd watched a load of old episodes of the TV series— both the British and Australian versions—so he could get the opening sequence just perfect and adjust the transitions in a way that would highlight Callie's familiarity with the programme, and therefore her suitability for the position she was applying for.

She spun to him now, her hands clasped beneath her chin. 'Thank you *so much*. This is a hundred times better than I could've managed on my own.'

In that moment he didn't begrudge a single second he'd spent on the project. 'It was a pleasure.'

'All that's missing…'

Her sigh had his gut clenching. All that was missing was the identity of her father. He wished he could give her the answer.

'But this—' she gestured to his computer '—is fabulous.' The corners of her mouth turned mock woeful. 'You do know they're going to ask me who put this together and then thank me nicely for applying and come headhunting *you*.'

He laughed. 'They're going to take one look at your video and have you signing on the dotted line before you can say *Mystery Family Trees*. Once you get the job, do you know where you'll—?'

'I've tracked Richard down,' she blurted out.

He fell down into the chair beside her. *'What?'*

'He lives in Larchmont.'

Larchmont was less than an hour's train ride away. 'Have you contacted him?'

'Not yet.'

A hard stone lodged in his chest. 'But you plan to?'

Her eyes implored him to understand. 'It's my last chance.'

He wanted to argue against it—wanted to order her to stay away from the man. Except, of course, he had no right to do any such thing.

'Frances's letters haven't shed any light on the subject?'

Her gaze slid away and her shoulders tensed as she shook her head. He'd be lying if he said he wasn't curious about the contents of those letters, but he refused to pry or force a confidence. On the surface Callie acted bright and breezy and cheerful, not to mention maddeningly capable, but every now and again he glimpsed her bafflement, her hurt, and her worry. It had his every protective instinct roaring to life.

'The man sounds like a real piece of work, Callie. He might not even talk to you.'

'I know. It's just… I feel I have to at least try to follow every possible lead…give myself every possible chance of discovering the truth. Even if it means meeting with people I'm convinced I won't like.'

Her life had been turned on its head when she'd lost her job—and not just her job but her boyfriend too. And then being given the news of her grandmother's death—a grandmother she hadn't known existed…

He understood her need to regain some control, and he admired her for shifting her focus and striving to win her dream job. She was determined to come back bigger, better and stronger. And he wanted to help her.

'He might try to extort money from you in return for information.'

Her nose curled. 'I hadn't considered that.'

He leaned towards her, sandwiching her hands lightly between his. 'Don't go alone. Let me come with you.'

Her relief was palpable. 'I was hoping you'd say that. I'd really appreciate it. I wasn't going to ask…you've done so much already—'

'We're friends, Callie. It's what friends do.'

Just for a moment her gaze caught on his mouth. Her lips parted and her breath hitched and every red-blooded cell in his body fired to life.

She snapped away, slipping her hands from his. 'Oh, is that the time? I need to pop out and grab some bits and pieces for the party.'

She wouldn't meet his eyes as she rattled on about the chores she had to do, and he bit back a curse.

'Is it okay if I leave Barney with you for another couple of hours?'

'Of course. Is there anything I can help with?'

She shook her head, but finally sent him a smile. 'It's mostly under control. Everyone I've invited is coming. You will be there at seven to help me greet everyone, won't you?'

'You bet.' Her party was this coming weekend. He'd even found himself kind of looking forward to it. 'Do you want to have dinner here tonight?' They'd fallen into the habit of her eating with him most evenings. He tried to keep his voice casual. 'It won't be anything fancy—just pasta.'

Her eyes dropped again. 'Thanks, Owen, but not tonight. Barney and I are having a quiet night in. I need to wash my hair.'

It was for the best. He knew it was. But that didn't stop him wishing otherwise or having to fight the urge to change her mind. He—

'Owen?'

He dropped back with a thud. 'Sorry, what were you saying?'

Her smile was gentle. 'Just thanking you again for… that.' She gestured to his computer.

'No problem at all. I'll see you later, Callie.' He pulled his chair across to the computer and opened a work file. He didn't glance at her again. 'You can let yourself out, right?'

'Right,' she echoed.

She was right. They needed to start spending less time together, not more. If he wasn't careful, when Callie left New York he'd find a hole had been left in his life—one he'd never be able to fill—and he wasn't opening himself up to that kind of heartache. Neither he nor Callie needed trouble.

* * *

Owen glanced around Callie's apartment, alive with music and people, chatter and laughter.

'So, after I'd read the letter she slid beneath the door,' Stuart was saying, 'I felt that darned ashamed of myself that I did a whip-around and we bought her that plant as a housewarming gift.'

A large cheese plant in a cheery white pot, with a big yellow polka dot ribbon tied around its base, sat in pride of place on a low table by the front door.

Stu was the third person that evening to tell him about the letter. Apparently Callie had written to each of the residents, informing them of the deal she'd made with Owen in relation to the apartment block, assuring them that nothing would change. She'd done it in plain, unadorned English, without fuss or fanfare, and she couldn't have found a better way to endear herself to the little community.

Stu pointed. 'Look, there's Angus.' He waved over the proprietor of the local bar, The Three Bells.

Owen stared at him. 'How do you know Callie?'

Angus clapped him on the shoulder. 'She's been unofficially tutoring Micah and some of her pals in the afternoons.'

Micah from the park was Angus's daughter? How had he never made the connection?

'And in return I've been plying her with some of New York's finest craft ales.'

That made him laugh. 'You've discovered her fondness for beer?'

'She has a very discerning palate,' he said with a grin, glancing around. 'Micah and her friends should be here somewhere.' He lifted his hand in a wave when he spotted them. 'I promised Lian I wouldn't let them stay out too late.'

Stu and Angus ambled off to top up their drinks. Owen glanced over at Josephine, Eliza and Betty, but they were in animated discussion with Claude and Jilly from down-stairs. So he made his way across to Mr Singh, who sat on the sofa with Barney.

'How are you holding up, Mr S?' he asked, lowering himself down beside the older man carefully, so as to not jolt him. It was only his second day out of hospital. Both he and Callie were keeping a close eye on him, not want-ing him to wear himself out.

'It's done these old bones good to come out to a party. It's been a long time…' He trailed off. 'She's a grand girl.'

He followed the older man's gaze to where Callie was busy refreshing her guests' drinks. She wore a dark red dress that was neither showy nor racy, but still somehow managed to shout exuberance and good cheer. When she turned too quickly the skirt would flare out, giving beguil-ing glimpses of her thighs. Owen had spent a significant portion of his evening doing his best not to notice. Like-wise, he tried to ignore how the line of buttons that went from the vee of her neckline to mid-thigh made his fin-gers tingle.

'She's promised to come walking with me and Barney every day.' He ruffled the dog's ears. 'She says she misses him. I know it's just an excuse. She has a kind heart. But she shouldn't be wasting her time on an old man like me.'

'Don't let her hear you saying that. She doesn't con-sider spending time with you and Barney a hardship. She likes you. You'll be short-changing her and yourself if you think otherwise.'

'Ah, lad, you've a kind heart too. You and Callie are two of a kind.'

Something squeezed tight in Owen's chest—something hot and sweet and intense and gentle and carnal all at the same time.

He glanced at Callie and his mouth went dry. Straight-ening, he stared about the apartment—really stared. While it couldn't be denied that the new coat of paint had freshened it up, everything else remained the same—the configuration of the furniture, the ornaments and vases and knick-knacks, the pictures on the walls—and yet the apartment seemed completely different. *Transformed*. And that was due to its new occupant. Callie had a life and vitality that infused the place, as well as the people around her.

Yearning drilled through him. Not just the hot edge of desire and attraction, but something quieter and stronger. The pulse in his throat started to pound. The longer he gazed at her, the clearer everything became. Frances had been imprisoned by fear and regret. Wasn't he in danger of making the same mistake?

A woman had betrayed his trust and he'd allowed that one act to cast him adrift on an ocean of suspicion and mistrust. Even though he knew Callie wasn't like Fiona, wasn't after his money or the financial security he could give her, he continued to hold tight to his…his *prejudice*—he couldn't think what else to call it—because it had helped him to feel safe.

His hands clenched and unclenched. Safety hadn't brought Frances happiness.

The hardness he'd been carrying like a ball of concrete inside him melted now, as if it were nothing but wax, spreading warmth and a new sense of possibility through him.

He wanted Callie—and not just for a fling. Finally he had the courage to admit that to himself. He didn't want to lose her when she started her new job. And…wouldn't that job mean she'd be based in the States? Between research trips she'd have to live somewhere, so why not right here, where she'd already formed a community?

He didn't have a crystal ball. He couldn't predict where things between them might lead. But instinct told him that if he didn't fight for Callie now he'd regret it for the rest of his life. He trusted his instincts again now, with a fierceness he refused to dismiss.

Callie glanced up when the apartment door opened and a bubble of something light and happy rose through her when she saw it was Owen, returning after having organised cabs for the last of the partygoers. She'd been aware of him all evening—intensely aware—and her awareness didn't dissipate now, even though the crowd had.

He grinned, and she did her best to keep her feet on the ground and not float up towards the ceiling.

'Your librarian friends are going to have sore heads tomorrow,' he said.

She concentrated on collecting up paper plates to put in the recycling. 'So are a few people in the apartment block. I'll be tiptoeing around in the morning, so I don't disturb Jean below.'

She straightened and pressed her hands into the small of her back. She'd been on her feet all evening, and felt as if she hadn't stopped. Yet when Owen looked at her like that—all warmth and admiration—energy flowed back into her limbs and she swore she could dance till dawn.

'It went well, don't you think? Most people seemed to have a nice time.'

He laughed and started gathering up glasses. 'Callie, it was a major success. Everyone had a ball. I can't remember the last time I was in a room with that many people who all looked happy to be there. How many guests did you have—forty...fifty?'

'Give or take.' She rolled her eyes in mock exasperation. 'When was the last time you were actually in a room with forty or fifty people?'

He paused, consternation chasing across his face.

'Hey...' She almost reached out to touch his arm, but that seemed unwise. 'I was only joking.'

He shook himself. 'It's a long time since I've been to a party.'

'They're not really your thing, huh?' She'd sensed that the moment she'd told him she was throwing one, but he hadn't complained or tried to get out of it. He'd been a good sport.

'I enjoyed this one, though.'

She found herself dangerously happy about that.

They cleaned the apartment in silence for a bit. When she told him he didn't have to help, he waved her protests aside. She didn't protest again. She liked having him here.

'What was the last party you did go to?' she asked eventually.

He tied a knot in the top of the last garbage bag before turning back to face her. 'My engagement party.'

Gah! Talk about putting her foot in it.

His eyebrow lifted. 'You?'

'Oh...um...a few colleagues at the university threw a leaving party for me.' She grimaced. 'It wasn't the best party I've ever been to. I wasn't exactly in a party mood at the time.' She moistened dry lips. 'I'm sorry about your engagement, Owen.' She dug out a smile. 'Would you like a beer?' She'd been careful not to drink too much tonight. 'I think we've earned one.'

'Sure.'

They collapsed on the sofa, side by side, and in unison kicked their shoes off and lifted their feet to the coffee table.

He took the top off her beer and handed it to her. 'The fact I enjoyed tonight's party more than my own engagement party probably tells you all you need to know.'

'Like you said before, at least, unlike Frances, you didn't marry your mistake. And I can't tell you how glad I am I kicked my own mistake to the kerb back in Australia.'

They clinked bottles and drank.

'You want to know something odd? Tonight I realised I wasn't angry any more. Somewhere along the line I've chalked Fiona up to experience.'

She stared at him. *Really?* How had he done that? She was still fuming about Dominic. 'What happened between the two of you?' She held her breath and waited. If he didn't want to talk about it, she wouldn't pursue it.

He stilled, a strange light in his eyes. 'You really want to know?'

With a dry mouth, she nodded. 'But, I mean, if you don't want to talk about it…'

'I'm happy to share the gory details, if you're interested.'

Had she imagined the inflection on the word *interested*?

'It started out much the same as a lot of relationships, I guess. We met through mutual friends and hit it off. She's one of those impossibly beautiful society women—polished, charming, always knows what to say.'

'I hate her already.'

He chuckled.

Callie tried to not stare. His mouth had lost the hard edge it usually wore when he spoke of his ex. 'How did you find her out?'

'I startled her one afternoon. I walked into the apartment we shared and she closed the lid of her laptop a bit too quickly, as if she didn't want me to see what she'd been reading. It sent alarm bells off in my head.' He pursed his lips. 'It wasn't the first time, and I couldn't shake the feeling something was…off. Anyway, the doorbell rang and it was her bridesmaids, and they all went off for a dress fitting. When she was gone, I had a look at her browsing history.'

What on earth had he found that could have damned the other woman so completely? 'What did you find?'

'She'd been researching the best lawyers for divorce settlements.'

Callie's hand flew to her mouth.

'So I waited a couple of days and then told her that my business was in trouble, and as a result we'd have to down-scale both the wedding and where we'd planned to live.'

'How did she take that?'

'Went ballistic and told me if she couldn't have the wedding she'd always dreamed of she wouldn't marry me.'

'Nice to see she was so supportive!'

'I told her then that I knew she'd been researching divorce lawyers and settlements, and that her reaction to my supposed financial woes spoke volumes. That's when it got ugly.' He kinked an eyebrow at Callie. 'She isn't the kind of woman who's used to not getting her own way, and she let me have it with both barrels. Apparently the deal was she'd get my money while I got the satisfaction of marrying up.'

'Marrying...*up*?' Callie spluttered. What was wrong with these entitled people? Her mother had been right!

He rested his head against the back of the sofa. 'Apparently she planned to use my money to save her family's fortune. Once that was done she planned to divorce me—and take me for everything she could get, of course.'

'Of course...' she echoed faintly.

'A child featured in this plan of hers too.' For the briefest of moments his mouth tightened. 'She planned to get pregnant and...'

She'd planned to use their child as a weapon against him? 'Oh, Owen.' No wonder he was so damn gun-shy now when it came to relationships. 'I'm sorry. What a dreadful experience. I—'

'All I can see now, though, is what a lucky escape I had. And you've reminded me that not all women—in fact not even the majority—are out for what they can get. I find myself...weirdly grateful.'

'Which is better than being bitter,' she agreed slowly.

'And I've been meaning to thank you for something else too.'

She took a sip of beer, trying to ignore the latent power of his body that was starting to sing a siren song to her. 'Oh?'

'I had a good talk with Lissy and sorted everything out.'

'I'm so glad!' His half-sister was smart and sassy, and she'd quickly become one of Callie's favourite people. Besides their shopping trip, they'd also spent a day in the city sightseeing, plus had another two dinner-and-movie nights at Owen's.

'She was taken in by Fiona too—totally fooled by her. Until Fiona *"tactfully—"*' he made air quotes '—told Lissy that she was taking up too much of my time, was too demanding, and that maybe it was time for her to grow up a bit and stand on her own two feet.'

Callie's feet slammed to the floor. 'She did *what*? What a complete and utter—'

'I know.'

'I hope you told Lissy that any woman who treats her like that isn't worth your time of day, and is not someone you want to be in a relationship with, and…and…'

He reached out and squeezed her hand. 'I did. We sorted everything out. I've also promised to do my best to stop being such an overbearing, bossy big brother. We're good, Callie.' He squeezed her hand again. 'And that's because of you. Thank you.'

She should pull her hand from his. She should, but she didn't want to.

'So I've been thinking…' he started. 'If you get this job—and I think it's a sure thing given your video—'

'It would help if I could find out who my father is,' she inserted.

'Well, I've been thinking…you'd be based in the States, right?'

She nodded.

'Does that mean you'll stay in New York?'

Something in his tone had her lifting her gaze from the sparkly purple nail polish on her toes to his deep smoky gaze. 'I…I don't know. I haven't thought that far ahead.'

'Tonight I realised that in the month you've been living in this apartment you've built a nice little community here. It'd be a shame to uproot yourself and start over somewhere new.'

She opened her mouth. She closed it again. If she could live in any part of America… 'This tiny bit of New York feels a lot like home,' she said slowly, realising it was true.

With infinite care, he lowered his feet to the rug, something in his gaze darkening and deepening. He set his beer on the coffee table and then took hers and set it beside it. 'Good.'

Her heart tried to beat a path out of her chest. 'Good…?'

One strong hand lifted to trace her cheek, while the other slid beneath her hair to cradle the back of her head.

'It's very good, Callie.'

His thumb traced her bottom lip, sensitising it until her breath hitched and the pulse in her throat fluttered.

'Owen?' His name was nothing more than a breath of a whisper.

'I find I don't want to say goodbye to you, Callie.'

And with that his mouth lowered to hers and she lifted her lips to meet it, helpless to resist the pull between them.

She'd expected the kiss to be slow and sweet, becoming hypnotically drugging as it deepened. It was nothing of the sort. The moment their mouths met they both fired to life—as if a current of pure energy had passed between them. Immediate hunger roared through her. Hunger that demanded satisfaction and release. *Now*.

Her fingers buried themselves in the thickness of his hair as she tried to draw him closer. His hands went to her waist and he lifted her into his lap, so she could straddle him and plaster herself against his chest in a move that felt like utter perfection. The alternative was for him to push her back into the sofa and cover her body with his but, while she hungered for that too, she appreciated the autonomy this move gave her, the sense of control.

Not that she *had* any control!

Drugging kiss after drugging kiss had her losing all sense of time. Owen kissed her with a single-minded focus that undid her completely and had her holding nothing back. She dragged his shirt from the waistband of his jeans to run her fingers across the hot, firm flesh beneath, and he hissed out a breath before raking his nails lightly up her thighs, now exposed as her dress rode high. She had to brace both hands against his ribs as a tremor shook through her.

Growing too impatient with the buttons on his shirt, she tore it open, buttons flying in every direction.

'I like your style.' He grinned at her—a lazy uplift of his lips that momentarily infuriated her because it hinted at a control she could no longer boast.

Lowering her head to one flat male nipple, she grazed it with her teeth, wiping the smirk from his face.

He swore softly, his hips bucking against hers. 'Callie.'

She ignored him to turn her attention to his other nipple until, with another oath, he snaked his hands beneath her dress to cup her buttocks and draw her more firmly against the hard length of him, thrusting up against her. A sob was dragged from her throat as light burst behind her eyelids, and her fingers dug into his biceps to keep her from falling.

'Callie.'

She obeyed the command in his voice to lift her head and meet his gaze. Then he stared at the row of buttons that ran down the length of her dress and his eyes darkened almost to black. Her fingers tightened against his biceps when he licked his lips.

'Undo your buttons.'

His words were part plea, part command, and all sin.

He made her feel powerful and wholly desirable. He made her want to slowly undo each button—to unwrap herself for him—until he was nearly out of his mind with need and greed and impatience. But if she did that there'd be no turning back.

The tips of his fingers had slipped beneath the edge of her panties and they caressed her bare skin, sending ripples of pleasure radiating outwards and making the very centre of her ache with need. She wanted those fingers exploring further, to more intimate places, but...

'I figure you'd be less than impressed if I tore all those buttons off that pretty dress.'

'No tearing,' she panted.

He stilled, as if sensing her hesitation. 'Do you want to stop?'

'No, I just...' She shook her head, trying to clear it. 'I can't help feeling we should think this through more. When we were at Ellerslie we said it was a bad idea...' It didn't feel like a bad idea. It felt like the answer to all her prayers. 'But the minute I—'

She slipped her top button undone. She hadn't meant to, but her fingers, it appeared, had other ideas. Owen swallowed, and she almost tore open the rest of the buttons then and there.

His fingers tightened on her buttocks, as if he were trying to get a grip on his own wayward desires, but in doing so he only fed hers.

'Callie, I have no answers about any of this. I only know I want to keep seeing you. I'm attracted to you—there's no denying that—but I like you too. I trust you. When I'm with you I'm...happy. Knowing you has made me feel hopeful again.'

How could she resist that? How could any woman resist it?

'I know you said this was the wrong time for you to start something new,' he went on, 'but I promise not to stand in the way of your job. I don't want to stand in the way of any of your dreams. But if you're planning to remain in the States then I don't see why we can't keep seeing each other.' He hauled in a breath. '*If* you want to.'

They could...

'We can take things as slowly as you like. I've no desire to rush you. We can stop right now if that's what you want.'

She didn't want to stop. And everything he'd just said sounded perfect.

Her fingers went back to her buttons and she slid each one from its buttonhole with fingers that were suddenly sure. His lips parted with undisguised hunger when she pushed the dress from her shoulders to pool at her waist. If possible, the bulge pressing at the juncture of her thighs grew bigger and harder when she unclasped her bra and dropped it to the floor behind her.

His expression made her feel like the most desirable woman on earth.

'Utter perfection,' he murmured, his gaze caressing her skin before he leaned forward and drew one nipple into the heat of his mouth, suckling hard.

Callie cried out, arching into him, her fingers digging into his shoulders, urging him on.

'I only date exclusively.' He laved her nipple with his tongue, sending a cataclysm of delight dancing across her skin. 'If you can't agree to that then we need to stop before this goes any further.'

When he pulled her other nipple into his mouth, grazing it gently with his teeth with such loving attention, she surrendered utterly. 'When you do that, Owen,' she gasped, 'you can have anything you damn well please.'

* * *

Owen knew the exact moment Callie woke. He registered her sleepy realisation that she wasn't alone, the slight pucker of her brows and then the clearing of her frown. She opened her eyes and her smile came without hesitation.

'Good morning.'

Her husky morning voice could devastate a mere mortal, and Owen felt himself falling hard. Not that he had any intention of saying as much and scaring the living daylights out of her.

Instead he grinned back. 'Good morning.'

And then he kissed her, revelling in her warm sweetness and the way she pulled him closer, as if she couldn't get enough of him. He couldn't stop his hands from roving over her delectable curves. Not that he tried too hard to resist the temptation. They'd made love several times last night, but the way her clever hands touched him—a deliberate boldness and teasing flirtatiousness, mixed with wonder and hunger—undid him.

Nobody had ever touched him like that before—as if his body had been made for her hands alone. And he made love to her again now with a newfound tenderness, losing himself in her breathless sighs and the way she whispered his name. She cried out as she came apart in his arms and light splintered behind his eyelids as he followed her into a kaleidoscope of ecstasy more intense than any he'd ever experienced.

It took a long time for their breathing to return to normal. He turned his head on the pillow to find her curled up on her side, watching him. Late morning sunshine spilled into the room, highlighting the creamy warmth of her skin and the rosy plumpness of her mouth.

'Okay?' he murmured.

'Very okay. You?'

'Never better.'

She frowned, but it wasn't the kind of frown to reach her eyes. 'I'm happy.'

He reached out to trace a finger along her cheek. 'That surprises you?'

'I thought I might wake up this morning with...'

His chest clenched. 'Regrets?' Had he pushed too hard last night? Should he have given her more time?

'Not regrets. I was never going to regret making love with you, Owen.'

He was glad she called it *making love* rather than *sleeping with* or *hooking up* or any of those other less intimate terms. Because what they'd done had felt intimate—not casual or temporary.

'I just thought I might wake worried about the future and wondering if we'd made a mistake or feeling as if we'd rushed into this.'

'But you don't?'

'I just feel...happy.'

It was enough for now.

He forced himself out of bed and reached for his jeans, though he almost launched himself back into bed at the heat in her gaze as it roved over his naked body. Instead he concentrated on drawing his jeans up over his hips without doing himself an injury.

'Do you have plans for the day?'

She shook her head.

'Hungry?'

'Starving.'

'Then let me take you to brunch. Frankie's is the best deli in New York. They do blueberry pancakes that will have you thinking you've died and gone to heaven.'

'Sounds fab.'

'I'll head downstairs for a shower.' He pressed a kiss to her lips. 'Why don't you head on down when—?'

His gaze caught on the stack of letters on Callie's bed-side table. Callie's letters from Frances. *Unopened.*

He glanced back at her and she bit her lip, some of the light leaving her eyes. 'I just…' Her fingers pleated the sheet. 'I just haven't been able to.'

A burn started up deep in his chest. She'd had so much to come to terms with in the last few weeks.

'Owen, just for today, can we not talk about it?'

He reached out to touch her face. 'Deal. Today is just about you and me.'

'Thank you.'

Her smile was the only reward he needed. 'I'll see you downstairs whenever you're ready?'

She nodded, her eyes sparkling again.

He hummed all the way down to his basement apart-ment. And if he sensed his progress being noted by several residents in the block, it didn't perturb him in the slightest.

CHAPTER TEN

'YOU'RE SURE ABOUT THIS?'

Callie glanced across the serving of hot chips lying on greaseproof paper between her and Owen and forced herself to nod. She mightn't have much enthusiasm for this upcoming appointment, but she had every intention of going through with it and meeting Frances's second husband, Richard Bateman.

The last four days had passed in a bubble of exhilaration and bliss. She and Owen had spent most of that time laughing and making love. And he'd shown her all his favourite haunts in Greenwich and the West Village. It had been perfect—as if she'd suddenly remembered how to have fun again after a hundred years of misery and gloom. Which didn't make sense. So little of her life had been either miserable or gloomy.

She stole a glance at him. She couldn't shake a sense of unease—as if this thing between them was too perfect and couldn't possibly last.

Don't be daft! How can anything be too perfect?

She tried to calm the sudden pounding of her heart. She hadn't embarked on this relationship either too quickly or with too little forethought. Why should she have hesitated? Owen was ten times the man Dominic was. She *loved* spending time with him.

'Are you sure you're okay?' he asked. 'You're very quiet.'

She forced herself to smile. 'I'm fine. Just…taking it all in.'

They'd arrived in Larchmont ninety minutes ago, and Owen had driven her around the pretty harbour. They'd walked down the main street, with its assortment of boutiques, bakeries and delis. They'd taken some video footage—just in case. And now they'd settled on the grass in the park with a view of the beach to eat their lunch of what she called chips and he called fries.

The town was lovely—really pretty. The company was great. In fact, the company was the best ever. The sun shone and the air was warmer and more fragrant than she'd so far experienced while she'd been in America. But her appetite had deserted her. And, although he smiled, Owen couldn't hide the concern in his eyes.

An answering anxiety churned in her stomach. 'Look,' she started, 'neither of us is expecting to like Richard, but I can't see what harm he can do us. Besides, what happened between him and Frances took place a long time ago.'

'He could try to charm money out of you.'

'I mean to try to charm information out of him.'

'You think he has any?'

'Probably not.' She pressed her hands together. 'It just feels as if this is my last lead.'

You still have Frances's letters.

She pushed that thought aside. She hadn't been able to overcome her reluctance to read them yet.

'So I have to follow it through.'

'For the job?'

'And my own peace of mind.'

He nodded, and she knew he understood. But questions continued to plague her, and she couldn't help but wonder what would happen when she found out the answers. She wanted to know the identity of her father, and she wouldn't rest now until she discovered it. But just as importantly she wanted to find out what had happened between her mother and her grandmother all those years ago.

If Richard couldn't shed any light on that she'd resolved to ask her mother. How else would she be able to decide whether or not to keep the inheritance Frances had left her?

But… She glanced at Owen. If she didn't keep it, how would he react? He wouldn't be happy—that much was certain. But would it bring their perfect love affair crashing down around their ears? Would he make it a condition—accept Frances's legacy or else he'd break things off between them?

She rubbed a hand across her heart. Surely not. He'd never be that unreasonable. But, no matter how severely she told herself that, a part of her remained unconvinced. Owen had loved Frances as if she'd been his own flesh and blood. Callie couldn't compete with that.

'What if he does know something and you don't like what he has to say? What if he tells you your father is a nasty piece of work?' Owen asked.

They were questions she'd repeatedly asked herself. 'I fully expect my father to be wholly unlikable. Why else would my mother keep his existence a secret? But I'm no longer a child that needs protecting.'

He shook his head again, but his lips lifted and his admiration buoyed her. 'You must want this job really badly.'

She thought of Dominic, and the way he'd gnash his teeth when he found out that she'd landed his dream job. His face, though, was hard to bring to mind.

'*Mystery Family Trees* asks its celebrity guests to do exactly this. I mean the underlying premise of the show is to illustrate history on a personal level, as a kind of living and breathing entity, but it can become extremely personal for the person whose family is being traced. It can be uplifting, but it can also be shocking. What kind of hypocrite would I be if I refused to follow through on my own family tree, just because I might not like the answers I find?'

She pushed her shoulders back.

'I'm doing this for my own curiosity as much as to get the job. I've come too far to turn back. But I understand if you don't want to meet Richard. You can drop me off and I'll text you once I'm ready to leave.'

Owen reached across and took her hand. 'Sweetheart, there's no way I'm leaving you to do this on your own. I'll be with you every step of the way.'

His reassurance and the warmth in his eyes had her chin lifting. With Owen beside her she felt as if she could achieve anything. She was on the cusp of a new life—a new job, living in a new place—and she was falling for the kind of guy she'd only ever dreamed about. It was all there, just waiting for her, and she wasn't going to mess it up.

Half an hour later Owen pulled the car into the driveway of a large and very beautiful house. Callie's pulse thudded. 'It's not exactly a shabby pile of bricks, is it?'

'Larchmont isn't exactly a shabby little town.'

He could say that again—and Richard's house looked as if it might be one of the town's most desirable residences. It was a turn-of-the-century colonial mansion, with stained-glass windows, and a deep front porch that oozed charm and tranquillity. And then she remembered how he'd acquired this home—by taking Frances to the cleaners.

She swung to Owen. 'Remember the plan.'

His lip curled. 'Yeah, yeah. Be charming, be polite, find out what we can. Don't call him names, don't accuse him of anything, don't punch him on the nose.'

'He's in his sixties and you're in your thirties. You can't hit the man. Besides…' she turned to stare at the house again '…it's hard to know what goes on inside other people's marriages. You heard all that Eliza, Betty and Josephine had to say.' She said the words as much for herself as for Owen. 'It's obvious that Frances could be stubborn. She might not have been an easy person to be married to.'

His warm hand closed over hers and the smile he gave

when she met his gaze had her heart turning over in her chest. She was glad he was here with her.

'Do you always try to see the good in other people?' he asked.

'I...' Did she do that? She hoped so. 'Come on. Let's do this before I chicken out. The sooner it's over, the sooner...'

'You can continue your search for your father.'

'The sooner we can go back to your place for the pizza you promised me and stretch out on your sofa and...kick back.'

A wicked gleam lit his eyes. 'Or we could kick back in my bed.'

She sucked her bottom lip into her mouth to stop herself smiling too broadly. 'To...um...*talk*.' But she inflected the word *talk* with so much extra meaning those teasing lips of Owen's widened even further.

'Because I'm such a good communicator,' he agreed.

She started to laugh, and it helped to dispel her nerves.

He slipped a hand beneath her hair and drew her face close to his. 'Hold that thought,' he murmured.

And then he kissed her—a brief, blistering kiss that had her blood pumping and heat rushing into her cheeks.

He eased back, his eyes travelling over her face as if he couldn't get enough of her. He nodded towards the house. 'Ready?'

She pulled in a breath and reluctantly eased away. 'Ready.'

The moment the door opened and she came face to face with Richard she could see why Frances had fallen for him. The man had charisma, and even at sixty-one he was still ridiculously good-looking. His greeting was effusive, and he was all charm, but Callie sensed that his charm was too practised, too calculated...and beneath the glittering cheerfulness in his too-blue eyes she sensed wariness.

When they were seated with coffee and cake in a conservatory that overlooked the canal—a magnificently peaceful view—he turned to Callie. 'So you're Frances's granddaughter?'

She nodded.

'I will confess myself surprised by your email.'

Gut instinct told her to not prevaricate or pretend she didn't know his and Frances's history. 'Because of the way your marriage to Frances ended?'

'Precisely. But what you have to understand, my dear, is that one only experiences that kind of acrimony, that intensity of feeling, when they have loved greatly. And Frances and I did love each other very much.'

Ooh, the man was oily. But two could play this game. She leaned towards him. 'You know, that's what I thought. I saw the photos of your wedding and the two of you looked so happy.'

He pretended to wipe away a tear. 'We were, my dear, we were.'

She made commiserating noises. 'I only learned about Frances when, upon her death, I was informed I'd inherited a substantial fortune. I feel as if I've missed out on so much.'

His eyes gleamed briefly at the mention of Frances's money and she knew she had the man pegged correctly. He was a fortune-hunter, and if he thought there was money to be made from her he'd do all that he could to take advantage of it.

Silently she thanked Owen for insisting on accompanying her. Not that she couldn't have done this on her own. Of course she could. But his support made her feel less vulnerable.

'That's why I'm trying to put together as clear a picture as I can of Frances.'

For an infinitesimal moment, he stilled. 'Your mother never spoke of her?'

'Never.'

He gave a gusty sigh. 'Frannie was never the same after her falling-out with Donna. I believe it's the reason our marriage failed. I'd turned my face towards the future, but Frances couldn't help but keep looking back.'

'That must've been very hard for you,' she said, careful to ooze sympathy rather than call the man any of the names that pressed against the back of her throat. Beside her Owen shifted restlessly, and she put a hand on his knee to temper the frustration she sensed rippling through him.

'It was.'

He shook his head ruefully, but she was aware of the way those practised eyes assessed her.

'Frances froze me out. And I'll be the first to admit I didn't deal with it in the most mature manner possible.'

He could say that again!

She took a hasty sip of coffee. 'These things happen.' She let a pause stretch and then said, 'I know it's a lot to ask of you, Mr—'

'Richard,' he ordered smoothly.

She simpered, but threw up a little bit in her mouth as she did so. 'Richard. It's just…my mother has never spoken about that time at all.' She opened her eyes and knew she looked the absolute picture of naive candour, but she felt no compunction using such tricks on the man. 'I feel as if a whole part of my history is missing.'

'Of course you do, my dear.'

He reached across and patted her hand, and she had to steel herself not to recoil.

'I understand that Donna caused you and Frances a great deal of trouble?' She sent him her most commiserating smile. 'I suspect she never took you into her confidence, but…'

He leaned towards her—all concern and encouragement. She could almost see the dollar signs in his eyes.

'But…?'

'But she never told me who my father was, and I wondered if you…maybe…had any idea…?'

Her voice wobbled as she spoke, and this time it wasn't feigned. That took her off guard. Did she care who this man was on a personal level? Did she have some secret hope of forming a relationship with her unknown father?

As if sensing her inner turmoil, Owen covered her hand with his. She took heart at his silent support.

Richard hesitated. Then, 'Do you mean your father any harm, Callie?'

She followed her gut instinct again. 'Absolutely not! I hope… Well, I hardly know what I hope. But it'd be so very nice to meet him, and maybe even forge some kind of relationship with him.'

'It heartens me to hear you say that.'

Something inside her tightened. 'So you do know who he is?'

'Why, yes, my dear.'

Her head rocked back. Her breathing grew short and shallow.

He spread his arms wide. 'My dear girl, *I'm* your father.'

She froze. So did Owen. She wanted to shout *I don't believe you*, but she couldn't get the words out past the lump in her throat.

He nodded, as if sensing her disbelief. 'It's come as a shock, I see. The thing is, I was dating your mother before I met Frances. In fact, it's through Donna that I met Frances. Of course, once Frannie and I clapped eyes on each other…' He shrugged awkwardly, but beamed as if nothing could make greater sense.

He'd torn her family apart and *that* was all he had to say?

Callie's stomach rebelled at the coffee she'd just drunk and it took all her strength to battle the nausea that threatened to overset her. Richard had used Donna to target

Frances. It was unspoken, but implicit in his words. And Frances… Her head started to pound. Frances had stolen her own daughter's boyfriend.

'I suspect you'll want proof, and I'm happy to undergo a paternity test.'

She didn't want this man as her father!

'But, in the interim, here's a letter from your mother. I dug it out because I thought you might like to see it. I think it'll help dispel your doubts.'

She took the envelope he handed to her. With numb fingers, she pulled out the mercifully brief missive inside.

Richard,
A marriage based on lies is no marriage at all. You know the truth—you know the child I carry is yours. I beg of you, please do the right thing and tell Mother.
If you deny your child again, you won't be able to undo the chain of events it will set in motion.

It was merely signed, *Donna.*

Callie ran her fingers over the words. 'This is my mother's handwriting.'

She passed the letter to Owen. He read it in silence before handing it back.

Richard shook his head when she went to give it back to him. 'You keep it, Callie. Ask your mother about it.'

She folded it and replaced it in its envelope, moistening dry lips, feeling her heart pounding in time with her headache. 'You never told Frances the truth?'

'To my everlasting shame, no.' He actually sounded truly regretful. 'By that stage I was in too deep. I was in love with Frances—'

Liar. He'd been in love with her money.

'And she'd never have spoken to me again if she'd known

the truth. I'd already sworn to her that my relationship with Donna had never become physical.'

Her stomach gave a sick roll. 'Didn't Donna tell her?'

'I said that Donna was lying. And Frances chose to believe me.'

Callie's hands had started to shake. Owen leaned across and took one of them in his. She held on as if he were a lifeline. 'Why are you telling me this, Richard? You have to realise it paints you in a dreadful light.'

'If we're to forge a relationship, my dear, I understand that I have to tell you the truth. I have to be honest with you in a way I was never honest with Frances. I don't want to make the same mistakes that I did in the past. You have to understand that back then I felt I was in a no-win situation. If I'd told Frances the truth she'd have cancelled the wedding. And I knew Donna would never take me back again.'

You think?

'There was everything to lose. What was there to gain in telling the truth?'

'A daughter?'

He sighed a gusty sigh and it was all she could do to suppress a shudder. He hadn't wanted a relationship with her back then and he didn't want one now. He wanted a relationship with her inheritance.

'I'm a reformed character, Callie. I've wondered and thought about you every day. And here's my chance to finally make amends.'

'You're wrong.' She stood. 'I could never have a relationship—any kind of relationship—with a man like you.'

She turned and strode out without a backward glance.

Owen slid a homemade pizza onto the table, along with garlic bread and a green salad, but Callie made no move to put any of it on her plate. Not even so much as a lettuce leaf, though she'd barely eaten a thing at lunch. Her eyes had lost their customary sparkle, her lips drooped at the corners, and her pallor caught at his heart.

He slid into the seat opposite. 'Lissy claims this is the best pizza in all of New York.'

Callie started, and blinked before seizing a slice of pizza and piling salad onto her plate. 'It looks delicious.'

But she didn't start eating.

He grabbed a slice of pizza too. 'Callie, I know Richard's revelation has come as a huge shock, but you need to eat something.'

She shook herself. 'Absolutely.' She speared lettuce with her fork and put it into her mouth, chewed and swallowed. Biting into the pizza, she did the same—chewing and swallowing mechanically—but he doubted she tasted a thing.

She didn't wax lyrical about his pizza-making skills or give him exaggeratedly over-the-top compliments. He didn't need them, of course, but it was out of character, and he watched her in growing concern.

Her shock didn't appear to be easing. In fact, it was as if she had a ticking time bomb inside her, waiting to explode. All he wanted to do was pull her into his arms and tell her everything would be fine.

Except he couldn't guarantee that, could he?

When she realised he was watching her, she pasted on a smile. 'I'm trying to work out how best to frame this revelation in my little documentary.'

He tried to hide his horror. 'You're going to make that revelation public?'

'It'll hardly be public. It's just for the interview. It's not like I'm putting it out there on social media.' She thrust out her jaw. 'Besides, I've done nothing to be ashamed of. Making it public won't hurt me.'

'But what about your mother? What about Frances?'

She shot to her feet, fury suddenly glittering in her eyes.

'Why the hell should I protect Frances? After what she did to my mother...'

She strode away from the table, giving up all pretence of eating, and he did too. He watched her carefully, waiting for her tears to fall; ready to pull her into his arms and give her whatever comfort he could the moment she needed him to. This had been such a shock. It had rocked him to the soles of his feet. And it had to be ten times worse for her.

She stood with her back to him, hugging herself, and his heart went out to her. Before he could move across to pull her against him, she spun around.

'If you still want to buy the apartment block, Owen, then feel free to start proceedings. I'm not accepting anything from that woman.'

That woman being Frances, he presumed.

He did what he could to drag a steadying breath into his lungs. 'Callie, I know you feel betrayed, but can't you see that Frances was as much a victim of Richard's manipulations as your mother?'

'Really?' She folded her arms and stuck out a hip. 'Tell me how you'd feel if this situation ever occurred between your mother and Lissy?'

His head rocked back.

'What? You don't think it could ever happen?'

'Not while Jack's alive,' he croaked.

She glanced away. He saw the way her fingers dug into her upper arms and was afraid she'd leave bruises.

'Callie, both Donna and Frances were wrong about Richard—but, like you said, everyone makes mistakes in love. Frances paid a heavy price for hers.'

'She chose a man over her own daughter—her own flesh and blood. I wouldn't expect my mother to ever forgive her, and what's more I don't blame her. I don't forgive her either.'

'It's not your injury to forgive.'

She blinked.

'The harm was done to your mother, not you. But that's beside the point. I just don't want you making a decision you might come to regret once you've had a chance to mull things over and think about it with a clearer head.'

She slammed her hands to her hips. 'If I follow your logic, I should give Richard the benefit of the doubt too. After all, maybe he just made a mistake as well?'

In her anger, she was twisting his words. 'We both know the man is a predator—' his hands clenched '—a loathsome worm.'

'*Exactly.* And maybe Frances was too!'

With a superhuman effort, he reined in his temper. Callie was in shock and lashing out.

'Until today you'd started to develop a fondness for Frances. You know she wasn't all bad. She was duped by a cad who—' he searched his mind for a way to reach her '—stole her power.'

She pointed a finger at him. 'That's exactly what I'm trying to get back—my power. I refuse to let Frances or Richard or…or anyone else stop me from doing that.'

Including him? Was that what she meant? Was that what she thought he was trying to do?

'Dominic stole my power when he had me fired.'

'You weren't fired!' He didn't know why he yelled the words, knew only that he couldn't help himself. 'Your contract wasn't renewed. There's a difference.'

'A mere technicality!' She hitched up her chin. 'You want to know why he did it?'

She'd gone so suddenly still his mouth went dry. 'Why?'

'He applied for the same job on the Australian version of *Mystery Family Trees* that I'm applying for here in the States.'

He froze, presentiment trailing an icy finger down his spine.

'When he didn't get the job, I tried to cheer him up by

telling him he was an amazing researcher and a wonderful lecturer and that he already had a dream job.' Her lips twisted. 'I didn't realise how much he festered over that. Unbeknownst to me he took it as a sop to his ego, a meaningless banality that proved I didn't understand him. So he took my dream job away from me so I'd know exactly how it felt.'

Nausea rolled through him. 'What a despicable thing to have done. But—'

'When he finds out I've landed the job he coveted…'

Her eyes narrowed in what he assumed was imagined satisfaction, but a moment later she shook herself.

'My application needs to be in by the end of the week. I don't care if you approve or not, Owen, I'm putting what I found out today in my documentary.'

He ignored that. If she wanted to include Richard's shocking revelation that was her business, but… 'The TV job…' acid burned his stomach '…it *isn't* your dream job?'

She frowned. 'I never said it was. I just said I wanted it badly.'

He tried to get his head around what she was telling him. 'I thought…'

Revenge. His stomach dropped. This was all about revenge. She'd told him so in the lawyer's office the first day they'd met. He'd been a fool to forget it.

'So all this effort has been directed at getting back at a man who isn't worth the time of day rather than actually scoring your perfect job?'

She glared at him. 'It's about getting my power back.'

'This isn't about your power! If it was about power you'd be putting your best efforts into finding your *real* dream job—there's more than one university out there.' He felt himself go icy cold. 'This is about getting even. Which means you're hurting yourself more than you'll ever be hurting Dominic.'

Her nostrils flared. 'What do you know about anything? You've known me for a month. That doesn't make you an expert on what I want or need.'

'I know you love spending time with young people and helping them find their way forward, like you have with Lissy and the girls you've been tutoring. I know you like taking Barney for walks in the park because he always picks someone to demand pats from and that gives you an excuse to sit down and chat with a perfect stranger. You like connecting with people, Callie. Sure, you enjoy research. But for heaven's sake, you became best buds with four of the librarians you met at the public library. History is a living, breathing thing for you—not something dry and dusty and impersonal.'

Her mouth opened and closed, but no sound came out. She folded her arms and thrust out her chin, but the martial expression had started to drain from her eyes.

A hard ball lodged beneath his breastbone. 'And if you think you're going to get a chance to indulge your personal touch in this TV job then you're in for a rude awakening. You'll be working months ahead of schedule in heaven only knows what part of the country—probably racing here and there to find out the necessary answers. And as far as the producers are concerned, the juicier those answers are the better. You'll probably never even get to meet the people whose family trees you're tracing. You certainly won't be the one softening the blow of shocking or confrontational news.'

She stared at him, visibly at a loss for words.

His chest cramped, making his breath come hard and sharp. 'Are you still in love with him?'

'With who?' Her eyes widened. 'Dominic? *No!* Why would you even ask such a thing?'

'Because all this effort you're going to—it's as if you're seeking his attention.'

Her lips thinned. 'You couldn't be more wrong if you tried.'

'So it's about pride? He hurt your pride and now you want to get even and hurt his.' Couldn't she see how personally destructive that was?

Her eyes went cold and remote. 'You're starting to sound like just another man who's happy to tell a woman how wrong she is, how she's got her head into a silly little muddle, but never mind he'll fix it all for her—a man who's happy to steal a woman's power!'

He rocked back on his heels, the injustice of her words burning through him. 'If that's what you think, then we have nothing else to discuss.'

She paled, and he immediately regretted the words.

'I didn't mean that. Callie, I...'

She pulled in a breath that made her whole body shudder. 'I know you're not like that.' Some of the steel went out of her. 'Not really.'

What the hell did she mean, *not really*?

'I think you're angry because I refuse to see Frances through the same rose-coloured glasses you do,' she said.

He had to clamp his teeth against an angry retort. He didn't see Frances through rose-coloured glasses. He'd *known* her. And, despite what Callie thought, Frances had been a wonderful woman.

'You're judging Frances based on one mistake. You're not judging the whole woman. You're shutting your mind off to everything else she stood for.'

She gave a harsh laugh. 'You feel it's your duty to see her wishes through, but I'm not the least bit interested in accepting her blood money.'

His jaw started to ache.

'When it comes right down to it, Owen, who would you choose—Frances or me?'

The world felt as if it was suddenly spinning out of control, and he had no hope of preventing the collision that was about to happen. 'Do I have to make a choice? Because I will never be able to hate Frances.' His chest ached. 'So if that's what you're asking of me...'

'It's not.' She stared at him with troubled eyes. 'Yet I won't be able to do anything other than loathe her.'

The ache in his chest radiated outwards.

She pressed her hands together, swallowed and gave a tiny but decisive nod. 'I told you this was a really bad time for me to get involved with anyone.'

'What are you saying?' His words were nothing more than a croak.

Her voice wobbled. 'I'm applying for this job, Owen, whether you approve or not. And I'm not going to accept my inheritance. Can you live with that?'

He opened his mouth to argue with her further.

'One thing I do know for sure, Owen, is that I couldn't live with your silent disapproval and disappointment every time you looked at me. If you can't talk to me about Frances, and I can't talk to you about my work...'

'You're saying we're through?'

Her eyes filled, but her chin remained firm. 'I don't see that there's any other option.'

She didn't? He felt as if he'd been turned to ice.

'There's another option, Callie, but if you don't see it then you're right—there's nothing here worth saving.'

CHAPTER ELEVEN

A KNOCK SOUNDED on her door the following morning and Callie raced to answer it.

Owen.

She stared at him and her heart pounded in her chest like a wild thing. She wanted him to take her in his arms, tell her he was sorry about their fight, and kiss her. She wanted him to tell her there was another way, and that their relationship wasn't doomed before it had even started. She wanted him to tell her he loved her.

The revelation knocked her sideways. Her fingers closed around the frame of the door in a death grip to keep her upright.

He did none of those things. He stood there stiffly, staring back at her with eyes that burned—as if *she'd* dealt *him* a mortal blow when it was *him* who was trying to control *her* and *her* choices. Her eyes stung and her throat ached. She wasn't letting anyone take her power away again, regardless of how much she liked them—*loved* them.

His nostrils flared. 'I came to make sure you're okay after yesterday.'

Of course she wasn't okay! They'd had the worst fight in the history of the world and—

'Finding out Richard is your father must've been the most awful shock.'

Oh, that. Her shoulders ached with the effort of keeping them from crumpling. 'I'm fine.'

He looked far from convinced.

'I never expected to like my father and I was right. I never harboured any secret fantasies that he'd be a good guy. It's just now I know the truth.'

He shoved his hands into his pockets, his shoulders as stiff and uncompromising as the line of his mouth. 'I wanted to let you know that if you need anything you can still rely on me.'

Yeah, like *that* was going to happen. She folded her arms across a chest that felt blown open and shattered. 'Thank you.' She was careful to keep her voice neutral and polite. 'Is there anything else?' If he wasn't going to kiss her, she wanted him gone.

'I'm still the executor of Frances's will, Callie. I thought it only fair to warn you that I've no intention of sanctioning any decisions you make in relation to your inheritance for the next fortnight—to give you time to think things over.'

All the brokenness in her chest filled with anger and it felt good. 'Two things, Owen!'

His mouth whitened at her tone and she told herself she was glad.

'One: you don't get to approve or disapprove of my decisions. You don't have the authority to decide what is and isn't in my best interests. Who the hell do you think you are?'

His head rocked back. His entire body rocked back.

'Two: you have no say in what I do with my inheritance. You don't have an atom of control over it. *End of story*. It's mine to do with as I please and you get zero input in that. As far as my portion of Frances's estate is concerned, you *were* its executor. Past tense.'

It took an effort of will not to slam the door in his face. She wouldn't descend to that kind of rudeness. But, seriously, the hide of the man!

'So, what?' His eyes flashed. 'You're going to sell this building out from beneath me as a form of revenge?' His hands slammed to his hips. 'Because revenge is your MO, right?'

His words sucked the air from her lungs. 'My *what*?'

'Revenge…it's what you do. You're going for the TV job as revenge on Dominic. You're throwing your inheritance away as revenge on Frances.'

'Those things are different. And if you can't see that then you're an idiot—a huge, big, amazingly dumb idiot!' She might be above slamming the door in his face but she wasn't above slinging insults. 'Dominic *deliberately* undermined me—he set out on purpose to hurt me. Frances *betrayed* my mother. And in doing so some could argue she deprived me of my father. Mind you, I'm tempted to thank her for that…but, however you want to view it, what she did was terrible.'

Owen opened his mouth, but she carried on over his protests.

'What happened between us was a love affair gone wrong.'

He stilled.

'Neither of us is winning. Neither of us is getting what they want. We have a difference of opinion that can't be surmounted. *End of story.*' Every word was a knife to her heart. 'I can't help feeling the way I feel, and you can't help feeling the way you feel.'

His eyes burned but he said nothing.

'You're not *deliberately* trying to hurt me and I'm not *deliberately* trying to hurt you. After all, you can't help being a jerk.'

The pulse at the base of his jaw pounded.

'But I made a deal with you and I mean to keep it. If you want to buy this apartment block, it's yours.' Another thought occurred to her. 'Do you want the video footage that you created for me back?'

'No.'

Fine. 'Is there anything else?'

'Yes.'

She raised her eyebrow in *that* way, because she knew he hated it. And because it was better than bursting into tears.

'Your inheritance isn't blood money, Callie, and it's not an apology. It's a gift of love.'

She took a step back. 'Difference. Of. Opinion.'

She was careful to enunciate every word before slamming the door in his face. Because, apparently, she wasn't above that kind of rudeness after all.

Callie didn't clap eyes on Owen for the next two days.

'Which is exactly how I like it,' she muttered, kicking the apartment door shut behind her after returning from her daily visit to Mr Singh.

Dropping her coat to the floor, she unwound her scarf and dropped it to the floor too. It was *freezing* today. The weather in New York made no sense to her. Yesterday had been warm. Today was Arctic.

Ha! Hot and cold. Just like Owen.

Speaking of which…

'I don't care if I never see the jerk ever again.'

Which was a lie. A big fat lie. And pretending otherwise wasn't helping her feel any better.

Her phone pinged as a text came in—her mum, asking if Callie wanted a video chat.

She and her mother had video-called at least once a week since she'd arrived in New York. They'd been careful to skirt around the subject of Frances and the inheritance. Callie had mentioned that she and Owen had taken a trip to Cooperstown, but she hadn't mentioned Ellerslie. She'd chatted away instead about her impressions of New York, and filled her conversation with news of Barney and Mr Singh, the girls she'd been tutoring, Lissy…and Owen.

She'd not spoken with her mother since her visit with Richard.

She hesitated and then texted back.

Just logging on to my computer now.

'Darling,' her mother started the moment she flickered into view on the screen, 'it's so good to see you. I— What's wrong?'

Callie's jaw dropped. 'How do you do that? I haven't even spoken a single word yet. And I'm smiling!'

'Your smile is strained, honey. Besides, the apartment is a mess when normally you're so tidy. What really gives the game away is your coat, lying on the floor as if it's just been dropped there. I know how long it took you to save up for that coat, and how much you love it. So something has to be wrong.'

Callie glanced behind her and with a muttered oath raced across to pick up both her coat and scarf. Shaking the creases out, she hung them on the coat rack before returning to the computer.

'It's nothing,' she tried to say. 'I'm just feeling out of sorts. The weather has turned frigid here and it's making me homesick.'

From ten thousand miles away, she could quite literally see the blood drain from her mother's face.

'You've found out the truth, haven't you?'

That Owen is a jerk, a pompous prat…just another controlling male who—

'You know everything!' Donna's hand flew to her mouth. 'About Frances…about why I left and…*everything.*'

'Oh, that?' Callie waved a dismissive hand through the air. 'I've learned a lot about Frances in the past few weeks. But I visited Richard last weekend and he filled me in on the missing piece I'd been looking for. I mean…you *did* know I was looking, right? I know we never spoke about it, but you know me, and I figured…'

'Oh, God, you *do* know.' Her mother covered her face with her hands.

Callie bit her lip. 'Mum, I'm really sorry about what Frances and Richard put you through. I'm outraged on your behalf, but I'm okay.'

Donna pulled her hands away, her gaze roving over her daughter's face. 'You are?'

'I know it's not a pretty story, but... Hell, there's a part of me that feels Frances took one for the team. I, for one, am glad Richard wasn't part of our lives. We dodged a bullet there.'

Donna's mouth opened and closed. 'Then if that's not the problem,' she said faintly, 'what is?'

Callie folded her arms and glared. 'Do you think I'm a vengeful bitch?'

Donna straightened and her eyes flashed. 'Absolutely not! Who accused you of such a thing?'

'Owen.'

'Owen?'

'Well, he said that revenge is my MO, which comes to the same thing.'

Donna's lips twitched. 'That's not precisely true, honey.'

'Semantics.' She waved that away. 'He claims I only want this TV job to revenge myself on Dominic.'

She'd told her mum about the job with *Mystery Family Trees* weeks ago.

'Dominic is a pathetic excuse of a man who should be dipped in hot tar,' her mother said.

'And that I'm only refusing my inheritance to revenge myself on Frances.'

'You're refusing it?'

Donna's voice had gone faint again and Callie blinked. 'Of course I am. For the same reasons you are. I don't want Frances's blood money—' She broke off to bite her lip. 'The thing is, before I found out the full truth—that she stole your boyfriend and cut you off—I...I was starting to like her.'

She frowned again, remembering every word that Owen had flung at her. 'Owen said it wasn't blood money, but a gift of love…' She tried to push his words away. 'But he sees Frances through rose-coloured glasses, because when he was a boy Frances helped his mother get out of a domestic violence situation.'

'Frances did *what*?'

Callie shrugged. 'She's helped all the tenants here— they range from recovering substance abusers and domestic violence survivors to illegal immigrants from war-torn countries.'

'*Frances* has done all that?'

'The tenants were worried when I first arrived that I might hike up the rents.' Callie found she could smile again. 'But they know better now and we're all friends.'

'Frances left you the apartment block?'

'I know! It's worth a cool sixteen million dollars. Can you believe that? The price of real estate here is mind-blowing. She left me this building, plus five million dollars she had in a trust for me, and she left everything else to you.' She clapped her hands over her mouth the moment the words were out. 'Sorry! That just slipped out. I know you aren't interested in hearing anything about the inheritance.'

Donna stared at her. Callie held her breath, hoping she hadn't upset her.

'Frances helped all of those people?' she finally said.

Callie nodded. 'It appears she changed after discovering Richard's true colours. For the last twenty years she shut herself up in this apartment and never left it.'

Donna blinked.

'And she did good deeds. Though she refused to take any credit for it. She sounds prickly and irascible and…' She trailed off with a shrug.

Donna's face became larger as she leaned closer to her computer screen. 'Callie, tell me everything.'

So Callie did.

When she was done, Donna leaned back in her chair and let out a long breath. 'And all the letters I returned are there? She kept them? And you haven't opened the ones addressed to you?'

'I figured you'd kept them from me for good reason.'

'I love you, honey, and I want to thank you for your lack of resentment towards me...'

'No resentment—I trust you. And I love you too.'

'But I want you to open one of those letters to me—it doesn't matter which one—and hold it up to the screen for me to read.'

Callie did.

When she was finished, Donna blew her nose, dried her eyes and told Callie to put the letter away. 'I should've forgiven her sooner. I turned her into a monster in my mind and bequeathed that resentment to you.'

'Oh, Mum, I—'

'No, honey, let me finish. Hearing you talk about her reminded me of the things I once loved about her—things I'd forgotten. She paid an awful price for the trust she placed in Richard and I'm sorry for that...sorry for how much he must've hurt her. I'm glad she had your Owen and his family to give her some comfort.'

Callie's chest cramped. 'He's not *my* Owen. He's a jerk. Do you know what he said? That he wouldn't *sanction* any decisions I made in relation to the inheritance for the next fortnight. Talk about pompous. Not to mention controlling.'

Donna smiled. 'Do you think I was controlling for keeping Frances's letters from you?'

'No! You were trying to protect me.'

'And I suspect that's what Owen is trying to do as well. He doesn't want you to make a decision you'll regret.'

Her eyes burned and her throat grew too thick for her to speak.

'And after listening to everything you've just told me, I think he's right. I think the inheritance *is* a gift of love. Honey, read your letters and send me mine. Then think long and hard about what will make you happy before you come to any decision.'

Callie swallowed. 'Are you talking about the inheritance, the TV job, or Owen?'

'All of them, darling. I suspect Owen cares about you very deeply. Don't you? What do your instincts tell you?'

She wanted to shake off her mother's words, but she couldn't. She recalled with startling clarity the expression in Owen's gaze after they'd made love—the wonder, the awe…and the hope. It was an expression that had only deepened in the days afterwards, even as their connection had deepened. Yes, Owen cared for her. He cared for her as much as she cared about him.

'Send off your job application, because it won't hurt to apply. You can always withdraw it if you change your mind.' Her mother hesitated. 'I suspect getting your own back on Dominic would feel very satisfying for a brief time, but is it worth turning your whole world on its head?'

The answer came swift and sure and had Callie sagging in her chair. *No.*

She was jobless, she had a ridiculously generous inheritance, and she was free to go in any direction she wanted. The only thing she had to decide was which direction to choose.

She glanced across at the drawer containing Frances's letters. 'We'll talk soon, Mum.'

From his seat on the sofa Owen stared at the wall opposite as the apartment darkened around him, but he couldn't be bothered to get up and switch on a light. The dark suited his mood.

He'd made a rookie mistake with Callie. He'd thought

that just because he'd conquered the hardness inside him and was ready to embark on a new chapter, it meant Callie was ready to start something new too.

Because that was what he'd wanted to believe.

She'd told him it was too soon for her, but he'd refused to listen.

And then to storm in like some authority figure the day after their fight and tell her he wouldn't 'sanction' any decision she made... What the hell had he been thinking?

He ran a hand over his face, trying to dislodge the memory from his mind, but it had been burned there. Could he have been more patronising and superior if he'd tried?

He didn't blame Callie for not wanting to have anything to do with him. Taking her inheritance and the TV job were her decisions to make. He had no right to try to force his will on her or to take those decisions out of her hands.

His chin slumped to his chest. How could he fix this?

What he wanted to do was race upstairs, prostrate himself at her feet and beg her to forgive him. He wanted to pressure her to choose him. But in his heart of hearts he knew that wouldn't be fair. She needed the time and space to work out what she wanted from her life without input from any man.

But the one thing he could do was apologise.

His head lifted. He could send her flowers, with a card wishing her luck with the job application and apologising for being such a jerk. He'd tell her he understood that whatever she chose to do with her inheritance was her decision and hers alone...that he'd overstepped the mark.

He swallowed.

And he'd simply sign it *Love Owen*, and hope she knew he meant it.

CHAPTER TWELVE

OWEN TOOK A seat in Mr Dunkley's office and tried to shift the weight that had settled on his shoulders over the last twenty-five days. Twenty-five days since he'd spoken to Callie. Twenty-five days since he'd messed up completely and alienated her forever. Twenty-five days in which his entire world had turned dark and bleak and the sliver of hope that had taken up residence in his heart had died a slow and painful death.

He wished he'd chosen patience and the long game instead of losing his temper.

He wished he'd had the chance to tell Callie that he loved her—properly and forever.

And he wished to hell he could focus on anything other than the remembered shape of Callie's mouth, the sound of her voice and the fruity scent of her hair.

'Owen?'

'What?' He crashed back into the moment, registered the lawyer's wide eyes, and bit back an oath. He had no right to take out his dark mood on the lawyer. 'I'm sorry. I was miles away. A…uh…work issue,' he lied, forcing himself to straighten and look interested. 'What do you want to see me about?'

He had his suspicions. He suspected Callie had had a valuation of the apartment complex completed and that Mr Dunkley had been ordered to put forward a price to Owen. He'd pay it. Whatever price she wanted, he'd pay it.

Mr Dunkley glanced at the clock. 'It's just that…well—'

The door burst open. 'Sorry I'm late!'

Owen blinked as Callie burst in, wearing her raspberry coat and shaking droplets of water from her hair as she dropped both her coat and scarf onto a spare chair. Everything inside him fired into sudden and furious life.

She threw herself down into the seat beside him, and the scent of her hair engulfed him.

'What is it with New York and the weather? You can't call this spring. I swear it feels as if it should be snowing out there.'

He couldn't stop himself smiling, even as his heart ached with need and want. 'You should see what it's like in the dead of winter.'

She gave a theatrical shudder, but laughed as she did so.

His pulse pounded. He stared at her the way a starving man stared at a loaf of bread. He couldn't help it. In the same way she couldn't help walking into a room and filling it with warmth and laughter and goodwill.

He couldn't get enough of her. And seeing her freed him and oppressed him in equal measure.

Freed him because to see her was a balm to his soul. Oppressed him because he wanted her. He wanted to hold her, kiss her and tell her he loved her.

But she wanted none of that.

She didn't want *him*.

It took all his strength to drag his gaze back to Mr Dunkley.

The lawyer cleared his throat. 'Ms Nicholls requested that I set up this meeting to table a proposition—one I have every expectation you'll endorse, Mr Perry. It's an enterprise that will amalgamate a variety of initiatives—'

'Oh, for heaven's sake, Gerry, could you be more ponderous if you tried?' Callie broke in, rolling her eyes even though her lips curved upwards.

Ever since Mrs Dunkley had drunk too freely of the punch at Callie's party and forced her husband to dance up a storm on the dance floor, Callie and the lawyer had been on first-name terms.

'Callie, this is a business meeting, and as such certain formalities should be observed.'

'Tosh,' she said cheerfully, turning to Owen. 'Let me cut to the chase. I—'

When her eyes finally met his, her words stuttered to a halt. Her throat bobbed as she swallowed. 'Thank you for the flowers and the card. They were lovely.'

She'd thanked him already, via text message.

'You're welcome.'

They hadn't had the desired effect, though. They hadn't had her rushing to his door and throwing herself in his arms.

'Have you heard back yet?' he asked. 'Did they offer you the job?'

'Of course they did. The video you made for me blew them away!' She shook her head and waved her hands between them, as if trying to clear her head. 'But that's all by the by, and it's not why I asked you to meet with me today.'

She didn't want to talk to him about the job because she thought he disapproved. The thought was a knife to his heart. 'Congratulations, Callie—I mean it. I'm happy for you. You've worked really hard and you deserve your success.'

She stared at him and frowned, as if she could sense the hollowness in his heart.

He straightened. 'So what kind of *initiative* and *strategic vision* did you want to *table* today?'

Her lips twitched and her eyes danced, but she straightened too, folding her hands neatly in her lap. 'Owen, I'm setting up a foundation. I'm calling it the Frances Foundation—because I like alliteration, don't you?—and as Frances's godson, and someone who loved Frances dearly, I thought you might like to be involved and become a trustee.'

Her words made no sense. A foundation bearing Frances's name? You only did that to honour someone, and Callie didn't want to honour Frances. She loathed her.

He leaned towards her. 'What about your TV job?'

Setting up a foundation and running it took a lot of time and…commitment.

Callie couldn't stop the nerves from fluttering up into her throat, making her heart race and making it increasingly difficult to catch her breath. She'd spent the best part of the last month asking herself all the hard questions—what kind of person did she want to be? What did she want to do with her life? What gave her joy? Where did she want to live?

And, most importantly of all, who did she want to share that life with?

She'd discovered the answers to all those questions and she'd found a way forward—one she could be proud of. But it hadn't happened overnight. It had taken a lot of soul-searching, a lot of honesty, and that had taken time. Too much time? She dragged in a breath. Please, please, please let there still be a chance for them. She couldn't bear it if she'd lost all hope of winning Owen's heart.

'I turned down the TV job.'

He stared at her. He had dark circles under his eyes and his hair looked in serious need of a cut. But the swift keenness in his gaze told her she had his full attention.

'You did *what*?'

His lips—lean and firm—reminded her of all the ways he'd taken her to heaven, and the memories tugged at places inside her with insistent hunger. It took all her strength to focus on his words and not to reach across and press her lips to his.

'I've decided to do something different. Something I think I'll find more fulfilling. I mean, the TV job would've been interesting in the short term.' She could feel her lips twist. 'But when I examined my reasons for applying for the job I came to the conclusion that they were less than ideal.'

He didn't say anything, so she continued.

'On top of that, there was a lot of travel involved—as I expected there would be—but no time to really explore the places that I'd be travelling to. So, basically, I'd be living out of a suitcase and...' She shrugged. 'That's not how I want to live my life. The time pressures and turnarounds were going to be tight, and I couldn't see that there would be much of a chance for me to develop relationships with anyone. And, as my career counsellor pointed out, I'm a relationship-builder, so...'

She let the words trail off, feeling she might be babbling and getting off course. But the way Owen stared at her, as if he'd hung on her every word, had her heart crashing about in her chest.

He leaned towards her, bringing those tempting lips even closer. *Breathe*, she ordered herself. *Breathe*.

'You've been seeing a career counsellor?'

'I had some big decisions to make and I needed all the help I could get. She was great too—really helped me sort out my priorities.'

He stared at her for a long time and she found herself holding her breath.

'Tell me about the Frances Foundation,' he said.

She let the breath out slowly. 'Well, we know that Frances championed the underdog, and—'

'You don't loathe Frances any more?'

'No.'

The light in his eyes deepened. 'Go on.'

Her heart raced. 'With which part?' She'd tell him whatever he wanted to know in whatever order he wanted to hear it.

From the corner of her eye she saw Gerry Dunkley get

to his feet and leave the room, but she didn't bother calling him back. Owen didn't either.

'The Foundation or not loathing Frances any more?'

'Tell me about the Foundation.'

So she did. She told him how it would be set up to help unemployed youths find jobs or develop the skills they needed to break into the kind of work they hoped to find. She had plans to create industry links for scholarships and internships. With her mother's blessing, she was going to turn the family estate of Ellerslie into a retreat-cum-training centre.

'Your mother has agreed to this?'

His incredulity made her smile. 'Absolutely.'

'I… This—' He shook himself, as if to gather his thoughts.

She wanted to kiss him so badly it hurt.

'Okay, first things first,' he said.

He hauled in a breath and she had a feeling he was mentally counting to ten.

'What do you see as my role in the foundation? Obviously you want a financial investment, but—'

'I don't want your money, Owen!' *Oops.* 'I mean,' she amended, 'the *foundation* doesn't want your money. Obviously donations are always welcome, but that's not what this is about. I want… I mean the *foundation* wants,' she corrected herself again, 'your vision. You're the person who loved and knew Frances best. We want your knowledge of Frances to help us determine the direction of the foundation—to help us decide what programmes to offer, what strategies to take. There'll be a board made up of my mother, Mr Dunkley and myself, and we're hoping you'll join us.'

He didn't say anything and her chest clenched up tight. It was entirely possible he wanted nothing to do with her, regardless of the fact that she now wanted to honour Frances's memory.

'I understand you might want to take some time to think about it. Mr Dunkley has drawn up some documents that you'll want to read over before coming to a decision. I'll call him back in and—'

'Don't call him back in.'

She swore her heart stopped—before beating even harder and faster.

'This is so far from what I was expecting it's making me slow to respond. But it's unexpected in a good way.' He reached out to briefly squeeze her hand. 'A very good way.'

His words unfroze something small but vital inside her, and she found that she could smile again. 'What were you expecting?'

'For Mr Dunkley to name the price you wanted for the apartment block.'

'Ah, about that…'

Owen sat back and waited.

She moistened her lips. 'I'm not actually planning on selling the apartment block in its entirety. I want to keep the upstairs apartment—Frances's apartment—for myself. But that still means the other seven apartments are yours if you want them. The proceeds of the sale, plus the trust fund Frances left me, will be going towards setting up the foundation.'

He frowned and she winced.

'You hate the idea, don't you? It's just, if I don't have to pay rent then I can afford to continue living in Greenwich Village.'

The apartment was the only part of Frances's legacy she was keeping for herself.

'I think it's a great idea! What concerns me…' his frown deepened '…is how you will support yourself. Callie, you'll need an income.'

'Besides giving Ellerslie over to the foundation, my mother is investing a generous sum to cover, among other things, my wages.' She folded her arms. 'Though we're currently in discussion about what that wage should be. She thinks it should be commensurate with my university salary, but I don't need much and—'

'She's right.'

Glancing up at the deadly serious note in Owen's voice, she found herself swallowing at his almost-glare.

'You can't short-change yourself, Callie. I can already see how much time and effort you're going to put into those youth programmes—your research skills are going to be well utilised. Additionally, if you were to eventually hire someone else, because demand required it, would you pay them a pittance to do the same work you'd be doing?'

'Of course not. But at the moment this is all a risk. It's possible we could lose everything—'

'You need to trust your board to have the competence to judge the programmes you propose, as well as your abilities to implement them. You deserve to earn a wage that reflects that.'

She opened her mouth, but he held up a finger to forestall her.

'Also, I will never lie to you. If I think one of your programmes is too ambitious, or won't fly, or has issues that need to be ironed out before it can proceed, I'm going to say as much.' He smiled briefly. 'I don't doubt there'll be days when you feel you're working very hard for your wage.'

She couldn't speak as she allowed his words to sink in. Hope tightened her chest. 'Does that mean you're on board?'

He nodded. 'I'm honoured to be asked.'

She smiled then too. 'I can't tell you how glad I am.'

She did what she could not to get lost in his answering smile, tried to force her mind back to matters of business.

'I'm sure you must have a lot of questions, and I'm not actually sure I'm qualified to answer them, so we should probably get Gerry back in here to—'

'You're the only person who can answer the questions I want to ask at the moment.'

Her breathing went erratic. 'Oh…?'

He stood, but her legs had gone to jelly at the expression in his eyes and she doubted they'd support her if her life depended on it. She remained seated, staring up at him.

'Can I take you out to dinner soon?' he asked.

'I'm free tonight.'

The words were out of her mouth before she could think better of them, but she didn't care. She wasn't interested in hiding how she felt.

'Perfect.'

He leaned down, his hands going to the arms of her chair, bracketing her in.

'Can I kiss you?'

'I think I'll die if you don't.'

His lips descended with a speed that made her head reel, but those lips—sure and tantalising, full of hunger and tenderness in equal measure—had her finding the balance she'd been lacking ever since she'd slammed her apartment door in his face twenty-five days ago, and she kissed him back with every ounce of yearning and need in her soul.

A short while later she found herself in Owen's lap on Mr Dunkley's Chesterfield sofa. She lifted her head and sucked in a breath, tried to cool the heat rampaging through her veins.

'Owen, we can't make out on Gerry's sofa.'

He sucked in a breath too, staring up at the ceiling for a moment as if trying to gather himself. He glanced at her, started to speak, but broke off whatever it was he'd started to say.

He grinned at her instead. 'Marry me.'

A laugh pressed against the back of her throat. 'Careful, Owen, you almost sound serious.'

'Because I almost am.'

She glanced back at him to find he'd sobered. Those intense grey eyes stared at her as if she were a miracle.

'I love you, Callie. These last twenty-five days without you have been hell.'

He'd been counting the days too?

'I never want to lose you again. I'm sorry about our fight. I'm sorry I overstepped the mark like I did. I panicked, and I know it's no excuse, but—'

She pressed her fingers to his mouth to stem the flow of his words. 'I'm sorry about our fight too. But you were right in what you said to me. I'd become too focussed on how people had done me wrong and on getting my own back. You held up a mirror and I didn't like what I saw. I didn't want to be that vengeful person.'

'Both Frances and Dominic injured you and—'

'And both of them are more than that single act. And in Frances's case she paid so heavily for her mistake and regretted it so much.' She pulled in a breath. 'I finally read her letters. She didn't reveal the identity of my father in them—she respected my mother's wishes on that—but through those letters I've come to know the woman you loved. And I've discovered that I like her.'

His hands cradled her face. 'I'm glad.'

'And in helping me sort through my own emotions, my mother has been on a similar journey. It's been good for the both of us.'

'I hardly know what to say.'

She smiled at him, love welling inside her. 'You've said enough for the moment. You need to listen to me for a little while instead.'

She straightened in his lap until they were eye to eye.

'I'm sorry it took me so long to work things out. Every

night I wanted to race downstairs and climb into your bed—I missed you every waking second.' She grimaced. 'Every sleeping second too.'

His arms tightened about her, and it gave her the courage to continue.

'But I knew it wasn't fair to come to you without a plan. I needed to sort my life out before I did that, and I couldn't ask anybody else to do it for me. I had to do it on my own.'

'I understand, Callie.'

'I have my work—my vocation—all sorted out now. I'm so excited about the Frances Foundation. And I know where I want to live—and that's here in the Village. You're right. I've built a community here, even in such a short time. It probably sounds crazy, but this place feels like home.'

'It's where you belong.'

'And I know who I want to spend my life with—and that's you, Owen. I love you.' Her smile widened at the awe and amazement that spread through his eyes. 'I love you and I want to build a life with you.'

His lips slammed to hers and he kissed her with a possessive thoroughness that left her giddy and breathless.

He lifted his head, breathing hard, his eyes dark, but a hint of humour lightened the corners of his mouth. 'I can't promise that I'll never be a jerk again.'

'That's okay. I'll love you even when you're being a jerk.' She sobered. 'I know that what you saw when you were a little boy—your father's violence—has affected you. I know that as a result you try to protect every woman in your circle. It's an admirable trait.'

'But I take it too far sometimes.'

'Owen, we're both works in progress. We'll work on it together.' He smiled, and a bubble of lightness and fizz built at the centre of her. 'You need to know that I'm never going to like baseball.'

'You don't have to like baseball.'

'But you love it more than life itself. You said so.'

'I love you more.'

She couldn't wipe the grin from her face, but a thought had her sobering. 'In terms of money, I'm not ever going to be rich. I'm sorry if that's not what you think Frances wanted. But in my heart I feel this is the right thing to do. I'm simply taking what she started and building on it.'

'I think what you're doing is perfect.'

She released a pent-up breath. 'So you don't care that I'm not going to be rich? And you know that I'm not after your money, right?'

'I know you're not after my money, sweetheart. Besides, you're already rich in all the ways that matter.' His hand snaked beneath her hair to cradle her skull. 'And I'm going to cherish you every single day of your life.'

'You are too, you know—rich in all the ways that matter. I don't want you ever doubting that.' She cupped his face. 'I want you to know that if you were to lose your fortune overnight it wouldn't make any difference to the way I feel about you.' She pressed a hand to his heart. 'It's the man you are, and your heart, that I love. And I promise you I mean to take very good care of it.'

'I know you will.' His grin hooked up one corner of his mouth. 'Does that mean you'll marry me?'

She had every intention of marrying him. But she wanted him to be one hundred per cent certain before she gave him an answer.

She stuck her nose in the air. 'Do you have a ring?'

'Not yet.'

'Ask me again when you have a ring.'

He immediately set her on her feet. 'Right, let's go buy you a ring.'

Her laugh bubbled up from the very centre of her. 'I'd rather stay here and make out.'

She found herself back in his lap on the sofa again.

'Good idea.'

'Though Gerry is bound to want his office back soon.'

'Nope, he took the rest of the day off—mumbled something about having to go home and kiss his wife.'

'Aw…he's a romantic at heart.'

'So it appears.'

She wrapped her arms around his neck. 'The answer is yes, Owen. I have every intention of marrying you. But this has happened so fast and I want you to be sure.'

He traced a finger across her cheek, his eyes filling with warmth and jubilation. 'I've never been surer of anything in my life. But I can see why you might think this has been a whirlwind affair. If it'll help set your mind at rest, you can choose the date of our wedding. I won't pressure you, Callie. I want you to be happy.'

'Hmm…' She pretended to think about it. 'I've always fancied being a spring bride. Do you have a spare slot in your diary next week?'

He laughed. 'For you, I'll find one.' And then he kissed her.

* * * * *

LET'S TALK

Romance

For exclusive extracts, competitions and special offers, find us online:

f facebook.com/millsandboon

⊚ @millsandboonuk

🐦 @millsandboon

Or get in touch on 0844 844 1351*

For all the latest titles coming soon, visit millsandboon.co.uk/nextmonth

*Calls cost 7p per minute plus your phone company's price per minute access charge